The Great Ghost Rescue

Eva Ibbotson writes for both adults and children. Born in Vienna, she now lives in the north of England. She has a daughter and three sons, now grown-up, who showed her that children like to read about ghosts, wizards and witches 'because they are just like people but madder and more interesting'. She has written five other ghostly adventures for children. *Which Witch*? was runner-up for the Carnegie Medal and *The Secret of Platform 13* was shortlisted for the Smarties Prize.

The Great Ghost Rescue

Eva Ibbotson

MACMILLAN CHILDREN'S BOOKS

First published 1975 by Macmillan Children's Books

This edition published 2001 by Macmillan Children's Books
a division of Pan Macmillan Ltd
20 New Wharf Road, London N1 9RR
Basingstoke and Oxford
www.panmacmillan.com

Associated companies throughout the world

ISBN 0 330 39828 8

A CIP catalogue record for this book is available from
the British Library.

Phototypeset by Intype London Ltd
Printed and bound in Great Britain by Mackays of Chatham plc, Kent

To Lalage, Toby, Piers and Justin

One

Humphrey the Horrible was a ghost. Actually his name was simply Humphrey but he had added 'The Horrible' because he thought it would help him to *become* horrible, which at present he was not.

Nobody knew what had gone wrong with Humphrey. Perhaps it was his ectoplasm. Ectoplasm is the stuff that ghosts are made of and usually it is a ghastly, pale, slithery nothingness – a bit like the slime trails left by slugs in damp grass or the mist that rises out of disgusting moorland bogs. But Humphrey's ectoplasm was a peachy pink colour and reminded one of lamb's wool or summer clouds. And then his eye sockets didn't leer or glare, they twinkled, and the sounds of his finger bones jangling together made a tinkling noise, like little bells.

His parents, who naturally wanted him to be frightful and ghastly and loathsome like all the best ghosts, worried about him quite a lot.

'I can't think why he has turned out like this,' his mother would say.

Humphrey's mother was a Hag. Hags have hooked noses and crooked backs and scaly black wings and when they move they give off the most dreadful smells. It was nothing for Humphrey's mother to smell of mouldy tripe, unwashed armpits and minced maggots in a single afternoon.

Humphrey's father would try to comfort her. 'Don't *worry* so much, Mabel,' he would say. 'The boy's probably a late developer.'

Humphrey's father was a Scottish ghost. He had been killed fighting in the Battle of Otterburn in 1388. This was a very bloody battle in which the English and the Scots killed each other in all sorts of unpleasant ways. Both of Humphrey's father's legs had been cut off by a cruel English baron right at the beginning of the battle but he had gone on fighting on his stumps until another wicked Englishman put a sword through his chest. Now he was called The Gliding Kilt because when you looked at him all you could see was the bottom of his kilt and then a space where his legs *weren't*. He was a very impressive ghost and a good father.

But the Hag, like most mothers, was a great worrier and she wouldn't be comforted. 'He's not a bit like George or Winifred,' she moaned.

George was Humphrey's older brother and he was a Screaming Skull. Screaming Skulls are just a skull with no body attached to it. If you try to bury a Screaming Skull it just screams and screams until you dig it up. They scream if you try to move them, too, or if anyone is coming that they don't like the sound of. In fact they scream most of the time and the noise they make sounds like seven or eight people having their insides pulled out so that someone who has heard a Screaming Skull scream is never quite the same again. Naturally this made them rather proud of George.

As for Wailing Winifred, Humphrey's sister, she used to glide about in a long, grey shroud trying to catch a little bowl of water which floated in front of her. The water in the bowl was for her to wash out her bloodstains. No one could remember how Winifred had *got* so bloodstained; she must have done something really bad before she died because she was certainly covered in the stuff. But however fast Winifred went, the bowl always went faster. Naturally this upset her so that she used to wail a lot, and that was why she was called Wailing Winifred.

They were a very happy family. There was probably not a more devoted couple anywhere in the world than the Hag and the Gliding Kilt. She kept all her best smells for him. He found her squinty eyes and long, black whiskers beautiful. Both of them loved George and Winifred. And they loved Humphrey too, very much – even though he wasn't horrible. In fact Humphrey, being the youngest, was perhaps just a little bit spoilt.

Not only were they a very happy family but they were a very lucky one because they lived in just the sort of place that ghosts like best. It was a castle in the north of England, with a damp, dark dungeon crawling with large grey rats, a moat filled with green, slimy water and a drawbridge which still had the hair of a murdered robber stuck to the rusted iron with dried blood.

The castle was called Craggyford Castle, so that Humphrey and his family were known as the Craggyford ghosts.

They lived very simply. Humphrey slept in a little

coffin under a yew tree in a corner of the churchyard and every night the Hag came to tell him bedtime curses and when she bent over him to say goodnight the smell of very old feet or extremely mouldy mutton would drift into his nose holes and send him happily off to sleep.

By day, of course, the children did their lessons. They had to learn how to leer, how to rattle their chains and how to pluck off people's bedclothes with icy and skeletal fingers. (George, who was only a skull and didn't *have* any fingers, had extra screaming practice instead.) Most of all, of course, they had to learn how to vanish.

Humphrey was particularly bad at this. He was the most patchy, messy, mucky vanisher you could imagine. Sometimes he'd forget a foot, sometimes a shoulder and once everything vanished except his stomach which was left hanging in the room like a round, Dutch cheese. Worst of all was his elbow. Humphrey's left elbow just *would not* disappear.

'You're not *trying*, Humphrey,' the poor Hag would scream.

'I am, Mother, honestly,' Humphrey's voice would come. 'It's just sort of . . . stuck.'

Winifred, who was a very gentle, kind girl in spite of wailing such a lot, would try to make things better.

'It doesn't really show up much, Mother. It just looks like a . . . cobweb or a bit of dust.'

'Rubbish, Winifred. It doesn't look in the least like a cobweb or a bit of dust. It looks like an elbow. Now again, Humphrey. *Harder.*'

But however difficult the lessons were, there was

4

always lots of time afterwards for them to do what they liked. There was a wood full of yellow-eyed owls where they played hide-and-seek, or they ran gliding races round the battlements. And of course they had lots of friends. There was Loopy Fred, who was a tree spirit and lived inside a hollow oak on Hangman's Hill, moaning and gibbering and waiting for people to come past so that he could turn their hair white overnight. Then there was the Phantom Sow who lived on Craggyford Moor. Pigs don't become ghosts all that often but this one had been hunted down and killed by no less a person than the second cousin of Robin Hood. Not that she was conceited about this: she was a very peaceable sow who liked Humphrey to scratch her back and enjoyed snuffling among the beech nuts just as if she were an ordinary farmyard animal.

There was also the Grey Lady who haunted the churchyard where Humphrey slept. Ghost Ladies, whatever their colour, are usually *looking* for something: buried treasure, or somebody they have murdered and feel worried about – that kind of thing. What the Grey Lady was looking for was her teeth. She had had a full set when she was buried – at least she said she had – and then someone had robbed her grave and this annoyed her very much. When you could get her mind *off* her teeth, which was not often, the Grey Lady was good at thinking of games, like Spillikins played with old toe bones, or snakes and ladders, using live vipers.

When you are leading a happy and peaceful life with your family, there seems no reason why it should ever end. Certainly Humphrey thought they

5

would go on living at Craggyford Castle for another five hundred years, or a thousand, or three thousand. But the world outside was changing. Life was getting difficult and dangerous for ghosts. Just how difficult and dangerous they didn't realize until one dark and stormy night just after Halloween . . .

They were sitting at supper. It was a simple meal but very pleasant: chopped rats' tails lightly fried in dripping, washed down with cold toad's blood. (People who think ghosts don't eat or drink or go to the bathroom are wrong. They don't *have* to but they *like* to. It passes the time.)

George had been naughty and screamed too loudly, and the Hag, who had a headache, had popped the tea cosy over him to keep him quiet. Often when you can't see you can hear better, which is probably why George was the first to stop chewing and say: 'What's that noise?'

After a moment they all heard it. The sound of horses' hooves pounding the air outside.

It came closer. A lot of hooves, and the jingle of harness, the creak of leather. . . . And then with a swoosh, and a gust of wind which sent the rats' tails skidding across the plates, an enormous phantom coach, drawn by four black horses, came racing through the window and came to rest in the air above their heads.

'It can't be!' cried the Gliding Kilt.

'But it is! It's *Aunt Hortensia!*' said the Hag, flapping her wings excitedly.

The door of the coach opened. Dressed in a huge white flannel nightdress embroidered with hollyhocks, a lady stepped out on to the dining room table. Above her rather grubby collar, her neck stump, a little jagged from where the axe had been, gleamed pinkly in the evening light.

'What is it, Auntie? What's happened?' asked Winifred.

There was a pause while Hortensia's neck swivelled round the room. It seemed to be looking for something. Then she dived back into the coach and took something out. It was her head.

'I have been turned out of my home,' said Headless Aunt Hortensia's head. It looked cross and sad, and its tangled, grey hair was all over the place.

'Oh no!'

'Yes.' The head nodded and a tear fell out of its left eye.

'Such goings on,' it continued. 'You know how comfortable I was at Night Abbey?'

Everybody nodded. When she was alive. Aunt Hortensia had been housekeeper to King Henry the Eighth at Hampton Court Palace. However, Aunt Hortensia was very bad at arithmetic and one day when she was doing the accounts she said that five plump capons, a flagon of mead and two tallow candles came to elevenpence three farthings whereas they came to elevenpence halfpenny, and Henry, who hadn't chopped anyone for a whole week, had her arrested just as she was getting into her bed in her nightdress and long woollen underpants, and cut off her head.

For a while, Aunt Hortensia haunted the Palace but it was so overcrowded with ghosts (three of Henry's wives were already weeping and wailing in the corridors) and she felt so out of things in her nightdress and long woollen drawers among the grandly dressed Court Ladies, that one night in 1543 she borrowed a phantom coach from the royal stables and drove away to find a place of her own.

And she found Night Abbey – a ruined and creaking house on the East Coast, with doors leaning on their hinges, bats hanging in disgusting clumps from the rafters and miles of desolate salt marshes for her headless horses to run around in.

'Four hundred and thirty-two happy years I've spent in that house,' Aunt Hortensia's head went on. 'And then three months ago . . .'

Three months ago, it seemed, a man called Mr Hurst had bought Night Abbey and decided to modernize it.

'What exactly does that mean?' asked Humphrey.

'You may well ask,' wailed Aunt Hortensia's head. 'It means washing machines in the scullery where my frogs used to live; it means fluorescent lighting messing up your vibrations. It means *central heating*!'

'Ugh!' The Hag and the Gliding Kilt shivered sympathetically.

'You may well say "Ugh",' said Aunt Hortensia. She stuck out an ample arm and they could see, where the nightdress had fallen back, her ectoplasm looking all dry and curdled, with a most unhealthy, yellowish tinge to it. 'I tell you, the place has become impossible,' she went on.

'Well, you must stay with us, of course,' said the Hag.

'It isn't just me,' said Aunt Hortensia gloomily. 'It's the same everywhere. Old buildings being pulled down, nice murky pools being drained, respectable ruins being turned into hotels or Bingo Halls. I hear poor Leofric the Mangled is haunting a *sausage factory*!'

'Well, nothing will happen to us at Craggyford,' said the Hag soothingly, piling rats' tails on to a plate for her headless aunt.

But there she was wrong.

Two

Aunt Hortensia meant well but she was *not* an easy person to have in the house. For one thing, she was terribly forgetful. She didn't just leave her head up in the bedroom when she went down to breakfast, she left it in the boot cupboard when she went out into the garden to pick Sneezewort or Deadly Nightshade and once, feeling playful, she threw it so suddenly at Humphrey that he dropped it and it said, 'Butterfingers!' to him in a very nasty way.

She would also get everybody very muddled up about what she was trying to *tell* them. Aunt Hortensia's neck stump had learnt to say simple things like, 'More please', 'No', or 'Pshaw!' but if she wanted to say something complicated with quite a lot of words in it she had to have her head. Being so forgetful she would sometimes say one thing with her neck stump and something quite different with her head. For example, if the Hag asked her: 'Would you like another toadskin sandwich, Aunt Hortensia?' the stump might say 'Yes,' while the head, on the other side of the room, was saying, 'You *know*, Mabel, that toadskin always gives me wind.' This kind of thing, if you have to live with it, can make you very tired.

But what bothered them most was that she was crabby about Humphrey. While they all *knew* that

Humphrey was not as horrible as he should have been, they really didn't want anyone else to point it out. Making personal remarks about children when you are staying in their house is not a nice thing to do but Aunt Hortensia did it.

'Really, Mabel,' she would say, disturbing the Hag as she sat in the kitchen copying curses into a recipe book or trimming the corpse candles, 'that boy of yours smells of new-mown hay.'

This made the Hag very cross.

'He doesn't. Not really. I admit that Humphrey has not inherited my best smells, but—'

'You're sure he *is* a ghost?' said Aunt Hortensia, interrupting her. 'He isn't really a Faery or a Brownie or something? I wouldn't be a bit surprised to find him creeping out at night and doing *good* to people.'

This time the Hag was so angry that she went through the roof. 'You have no right to say such things, Aunt Hortensia,' she said when she came down again. 'Why, only yesterday, when I was in the garden, I saw a chicken run in *terror* from Humphrey.'

'A chicken!' snorted Aunt Hortensia.

When something upset the Hag she always talked it over with her husband.

'She's got her knife into Humphrey,' she said that night to the Gliding Kilt as they were preparing to go to bed. 'Just because he dropped her beastly head.'

'We must be patient, dear,' said her husband, taking the sword out of his chest and putting it neatly on the pillow. 'After all she's had a bad time.

11

Have you noticed how lumpy her neck stump is looking? And anyway, Mabel, you *know* that chicken wasn't running *away* from Humphrey. It was running *towards* its mother.'

The Hag blushed and sent a whiff of squashed dung beetle across the room.

'Oh well.' She got into bed beside her husband and laid her hideous head lovingly against his gaping wound. 'Maybe we could spray him with something to make him smell bad,' she murmured sleepily. 'Pus from an open boil might work . . . mixed with sour milk . . . or smouldering Wellington boots . . .'

But when morning came, everybody had more important things to think about than how to make Humphrey smell as awful as his mother. Because that was the morning the men came.

There were a lot of men: four ordinary-looking ones in caps and raincoats who arrived in a blue van and ran about with tape measures and plumb lines and long, striped poles, and two more important-looking ones with fat, red necks who came in a big, grey car and had thick overcoats and notebooks which flapped in the wind.

They stayed all morning, pacing the grounds, jabbing at the woodwork with their penknives, shouting to each other, and when they went away more men came the next day and the day after that.

It was a great strain for the ghosts. They didn't know what was happening and of course with all those people around they had to stay invisible. Ghosts *can* stay invisible for days on end but they don't *like* it. It makes them feel unwanted.

12

Then the men stopped coming for a few weeks and everything was quiet again. But the poor ghosts didn't have long to enjoy the peace of Craggyford because what came next was the bulldozers.

'Mother, they're digging up the West Meadow,' said Humphrey worriedly. 'What will happen to those nice moles?'

But the men didn't care about the moles and they didn't care about the young trees in the Hazel Copse or about the blackbirds and thrushes that roosted in the hedgerows. They just bulldozed through everything and when it was all flat, dead rubble they began to build. And what they built was little wooden bungalows, lots and lots of them in straight rows, running towards the castle.

'Perhaps the army is coming?' suggested the Gliding Kilt, cheering up a little because he had been a fine and mighty soldier.

But it wasn't the army. What the men were building was a holiday camp, and the little houses were for the holidaymakers to sleep in. But for their meals and their entertainment, the holiday visitors were to go to the castle. And that meant that the castle had to be modernized.

'Oh that this should happen to me all over again!' wailed Aunt Hortensia, as the lorries full of workmen came thundering across the drawbridge. 'Twice in a lifetime! It's too much. My ectoplasm! What will happen to my ectoplasm!'

'It's the children's ectoplasm I'm thinking of,' snapped the Hag. Hortensia was getting on her nerves more and more, and those phantom horses of hers in the stable, eating their heads off – even if their heads *were* off already . . .

The next few months were desperately anxious ones for the ghosts. For they soon realized that it wasn't just central heating and strip lighting and bathrooms that were being put into Craggyford. No, the whole castle was being completely rebuilt. The nice, mouldering armoury full of owl pellets and cobwebs was turned into a restaurant with mirrored walls and a plastic floor. The Banqueting Hall, which had been the ghosts' dining room, became a disco-theque with terrible strobe lights which brought the Hag out in spots even in the few minutes the workmen were testing them. The lovely, dark, damp dungeons were tiled and turned into a gleaming, white kitchen so that hundreds of innocent woodlice and friendly spiders and harmless mice were walled up alive or turned out into the cold.

But it wasn't till George came screaming down the corridor to tell his parents what was going to happen to the East Wing of the castle that the ghosts realised how serious things were.

'A *cinema*,' cried the Hag. 'Are you sure?'

'Oh, I shall like a cinema,' said Humphrey, waving his arms about. 'Cowboys and Indians. Wicked gangsters. Bang bang!'

'Be quiet,' said the Hag, clouting him with her wing. 'You don't know what you're talking about. Films aren't like that any more.'

'What are they like, Mother?' asked Winifred.

'Rude,' said the Hag simply. 'Rude and shocking.'

'And that's quite apart from the litter,' said Aunt Hortensia's head. 'Iced lolly sticks in Winifred's bowl, toffee papers stuck to my stump, chewing gum jammed in our ear holes – that's what a cinema will mean.'

The Hag turned to her husband. 'Hamish,' she said, and her squinty eyes were desperate, 'what is to be done?'

There was a moment of silence while the Gliding Kilt stood twirling the sword in his chest, always a sign that he was thinking deeply. Then:

'Mabel,' he said. 'Everybody. You must be brave. There's nothing else for it. We must leave Craggyford and find another place to live.'

'Leave Craggyford,' faltered the Hag. 'Leave our ancestral home?'

The Gliding Kilt put a soothing hand on her crooked back.

'Think of the children,' he said.

That did it, of course. 'You're right, dear,' she said. 'Right as always. We'll leave at once.'

Three

They set off late that night. It was very painful saying goodbye to Craggyford where they'd spent nearly five hundred years but everybody tried to be brave. Loopy Fred came out of his hollow oak to wave to them and the Grey Lady cried. They offered to take her along but she said she was almost certain her teeth would turn up quite soon now and she didn't think anyone would dare to dig up the churchyard so she stayed.

Humphrey had hoped to be allowed to sit behind his father on one of the headless horses but his father took George, and Humphrey had to travel inside the coach with his mother and Winifred. Aunt Hortensia drove, of course – after all it was her coach – but she left her head inside because of the wind. Humphrey was never a very good traveller and this old, white-haired head rolling back and forward on the seat every time they turned a corner made him feel queasy very quickly.

'You'll have to use Winifred's bowl, dear,' said the Hag. 'We really can't keep stopping in mid-air.' But of course Winifred's bowl was for *washing* and she didn't want to use it for Humphrey to be sick in. It was not a very happy journey.

Although there was a moon, there was a lot of cloud with it and it was very difficult to see exactly

16

what they were flying over. Once the coach swooped down on what looked like a hopeful building but it turned out to be a steam laundry working a night shift. Once George screamed: 'Look, Dad, there's a nice castle!' but when they came down they found it was a huge factory manufacturing bathroom fittings.

'Disgusting!' said Aunt Hortensia, looking at the gleaming white baths and marble washbasins and gold-plated showers in the showrooms. 'All that washing humans do. No wonder they aren't fit for anything.'

They drove on for another hour and then they had to come down again because the horses were tired.

'Look at those funny black mountains!' said Humphrey.

They had landed on a large, sludgy piece of waste ground between an enormous, parked excavator and a mechanical shovel.

'They're not exactly mountains,' said the Gliding Kilt. 'They're big heaps of coal. We've come down on an open-cast mine.'

'Oh, dear,' said the Hag, who would have liked somewhere more romantic. 'Never mind, it'll do to stretch our legs.'

'I don't want coal dust all over my stump,' grumbled Aunt Hortensia. But she got down too and wandered off, holding her nightdress out of the dirt and splashing through the puddles with her enormous, yellow feet.

Humphrey was still feeling sick after the journey and the ball and chain which the Hag always made him wear on long journeys to strengthen his ankle had made him stiff and sore. So to cheer himself up he glided into the cab of the mechanical shovel and started making what he *thought* were mechanical shovel-driving noises.

After a bit he realized that the shovel-driving noises had turned into something different. Into a strange, low whining noise. A kind of *animal* noise.

When he'd made quite sure it wasn't *him* making the noise, Humphrey glided out of the driving seat and began to search carefully between the heaps of coal, now getting closer to the sound, now losing it again. And then suddenly, coming round a pile of scaffolding, he saw something that made him gasp.

It was a Shuk. A real, proper Black Shuk with a single, red saucer eye, huge, backward-pointing feet and three tails.

Humphrey was enchanted. Shuks are phantom dogs and quite rare now. He'd heard of them often but never seen one.

'Oh, come here, you nice Shuk. Come along. Good dog. Good dog,' said Humphrey, clicking his finger bones.

At first the Shuk didn't move. His one eye burned warily and he made a low, rumbling noise in his throat, like stones falling over a cliff.

'Don't be frightened. I'm Humphrey. Humphrey the *Horrible*. Come on Shuksie.'

The rumbles died away. The Shuk came closer.

'Oh, you poor thing! Why you aren't well at *all*.'

Humphrey was right. The Shuk was in a dreadful state. His tails were as limp as over-cooked spaghetti, his saucer eye was on the blink and his coat was matted and caked with grime.

As though he knew, now, that Humphrey the Horrible would help him, the Shuk came forward, making a weird, plashing noise as he walked. Two of his tails were wagging but the third was still a little shy.

'What *have* you got there, Humphrey,' shouted the Hag. flying over and peering with her squinty eyes between the heaps of coal.

'Oh, Mother, it's a Shuk. A proper padfoot – you know. And he's *miserable* here you can see. I expect this used to be a lovely wild bit of country and he'd haunt it and people who saw him would go mad with terror. And now he has to haunt this silly coal mine and have coal dust in his lungs and fumes from all those bulldozers and excavators and things. *Please*, can't we take him with us?'

'Yes, *please*, Mother,' said George and Winifred, gliding up to join them.

'Don't be silly, dears. We haven't got a home ourselves. How can we be taking in stray dogs?'

'I'm *sure* he'll be useful,' said Humphrey imploringly.

'Useful!' yelled the Hag, letting a burst of rotten pig's kidneys out into the night air. 'What can he possibly do? Now don't be silly, Humphrey. Come on children, back into the coach.'

Humphrey could hardly bear it. As he looked at the Shuk, gazing trustingly up at him, he felt as if his ectoplasm had turned to lead. They were all climbing sadly in when a wail from Aunt Hortensia's stump stopped them.

'Head,' wailed the stump. 'Gone! Gone!'

Everybody sighed and climbed out again, and the

Gliding Kilt murmured something rude and Scottish. It was not the sort of night in which you wanted to go searching for someone's old and smelly head.

It was then that Humphrey had an idea. 'Shuk?' he said. 'Here. Shuksie.'

The black beast bounded up and looked hopefully at Humphrey. 'Have you got a handkerchief, Aunt Hortensia?' Humphrey went on.

She nodded her stump and fished under her nightdress in the pocket of her long woollen drawers. 'Here.'

Humphrey took it and held it to the dog's nose. 'Find, Shuksie. Go on. *Find.*'

There was a pause while the phantom beast sniffed the speck of linen. Then his head went down and his three tails went up and with a noise like an underground pumping station, he was off.

Humphrey waited anxiously as the red beam of light from the Shuk's one eye raked the darkness. Then they heard him give a growl of satisfaction and pounce. Seconds later he had bounded back to the coach. And in his jaws, covered with black sludge but smiling happily, was Aunt Hortensia's head.

'That is a very intelligent and useful animal,' said the Head. 'I had rolled into a ditch and might never have been found.'

'You see, Mother,' said Humphrey, 'You *see.*'

Like all the best mothers, the Hag knew when she was beaten. 'All right,' she said, sighing. 'But mind you keep those disgusting feet of his off the upholstery.'

They rode on for miles and miles and still there

was no sign of an empty castle or ruined abbey or crumbling peel tower where a tired family of ghosts could come to rest.

And then, just a couple of hours before dawn, when the sky was beginning to look dark grey instead of inky black, the Gliding Kilt turned his head and said: 'Down there. What's down there?'

They all scrambled to the window and looked out. Below them, set in a big park, they could just make out the outline of a huge building. It had four towers, a central courtyard, battlements. . . .

'A castle!' cried Humphrey. 'Can we live here?'

'We'll just go down and take a look,' said the Gliding Kilt.

The horses were tired and glad to lose height. As they galloped round the building everyone became more cheerful. There was ivy creeping up the walls, some of the windows were barred; a fierce black crow rose squawking as they came.

'Really this seems very possible,' said the Hag. 'Look, there are two stinking serpents hanging out of that window,' she went on, sniffing happily. 'Let's drive in there.'

Aunt Hortensia had her faults but she certainly knew how to handle her horses. Skilfully she turned, and the coach drove past the stripy, stinking snakes hanging on the sill and in through the window.

Only they weren't stinking snakes. They were the football socks of a boy called Maurice Crawler who had extremely smelly feet. And what the ghosts had done was to drive straight into the boys' dormitory of Norton Castle School.

21

Four

Rick was usually the first person in the dormitory to wake. This morning he woke up particularly early because he had been thinking very hard the night before and the thinking had got into his sleep.

He was a serious boy with a thin face, big dark eyes and ears which stuck out because when he was a baby his mother had liked him too much to stick them down with sellotape as the doctor had told her to.

What Rick was thinking about was the world. The world, it seemed to Rick, was in a bad way. In the Antarctic, the penguins were all stuck up with oil and couldn't even waddle. Blue whales were practically extinct, no one had seen a square-lipped rhinoceros for ages and a tribe of cannibals in the Amazon jungle which Rick had hoped to visit when he grew up had been moved to a housing estate in Rio de Janeiro. It seemed to Rick that by the time he was grown up, all the interesting animals and plants and people would have gone and there'd be nothing left but huge blocks of flats and boring shops and motorways. The whole thing annoyed him.

He looked round the dormitory. Norton Castle had been built about a hundred years ago by a rich toffee manufacturer called Albert Borringer. Mr Borringer was one of those people who couldn't see an animal without wanting to shoot it and stuff it and stick it on the wall, and when he died and the castle became a school, the stuffed animals stayed. In the bed opposite Rick's, under a huge wildebeeste with mild, glass eyes, Maurice Crawler was snoring. What with his dimpled knees, hot feet and piggy eyes the colour of baked beans, Maurice was not really a great joy to anyone. On the other hand if it wasn't for Maurice there wouldn't have been a school because his parents were the headmaster and headmistress. They had started the school for Maurice because he hadn't settled in the school they sent him to. He hadn't settled in *five* schools they'd sent him to and no wonder. Maurice was a bully and a liar and a cheat.

Rick sighed. In the bed next to him, a new boy called Peter Thorne moaned in his sleep. He was still terribly homesick. Rick was sorry for him but he would have liked an ally. Someone to help him get things *done*.

Suddenly he leant forward. What was that funny pink, cobwebby thing hanging on the end of his bed. He put out a hand to touch it. To his amazement, his hand went right through and hit the end of the bed. And yet he could *see* something there. And then:

'No!' said Rick under his breath. 'I don't believe it. I simply don't believe it!'

Before putting him to bed, the Hag had ordered Humphrey most *particularly* not to become visible until she told him to. But of course if someone tickles your elbow when you are fast asleep you don't always think what you are doing, and the next second, rubbing his eyes and yawning, Humphrey had become as visible as daylight.

'What don't you believe?' said Humphrey sleepily.

'But you can't be. It's impossible. You *can't* be a ghost.'

Humphrey was not a touchy person but this annoyed him. 'What do you mean I can't be a ghost? I *am* a ghost. I'm Humphrey. The Horrible.'

Rick just couldn't believe his eyes. Yet there it was, sitting on the bed, transparent as air, with a ball and chain on its left ankle, rubbing its eye sockets with skeletal fingers.

'Who are you?' asked Humphrey. 'I suppose you're a human. A boy?'

'Sure. I'm Rick.'

'Just Rick? Not Rick the Revolting or Rick the Repulsive or anything like that?'

'No. Just Rick Henderson. Rick's short for Richard. Come to that you're not so *very* horrible, are you? I don't mean to be personal.'

'I will be later,' said Humphrey confidently. 'I'm growing into it. My mother and father are horrible,' he went on proudly. 'So are my brother and sister. And my Aunt Hortensia is really *disgusting*.'

'Oh,' said Rick. He still hadn't got over the fact that a real live – well, a real dead ghost – was sitting on his bed. 'Are they here too?'

'Oh yes, they're all here. We came last night.'

And he began to tell Rick the story of their adventures, beginning with the man who'd put central heating into Night Abbey, going on to the people who'd turned Craggyford into a holiday camp and ending with the poor Shuk who'd been found trying to haunt a coal mine. And as Rick listened he got angrier and angrier. Not just penguins and whales and cannibals were being driven out and made homeless or extinct but ghosts as well.

'It's disgusting,' said Rick when Humphrey had finished. 'Ghosts have as much right to be around as anybody else. Something must be done.'

'What?' asked Humphrey, looking at Rick admiringly. He already thought him incredibly clever.

'I shall think. Do you suppose I could meet your family?'

'Of course,' said Humphrey, gliding over to Maurice Crawler's bed.

'My goodness,' said Rick. From the fat hump which was Maurice's stomach there rose two huge, black, scaly wings. For a moment they flopped up and down while the Hag did her early morning stretch. Then they parted to show a huge, crooked nose, squinty eyes and masses of black and tangled hair. At the same time, the smell of burnt tripe crept sickeningly into Rick's nose.

'This is my mother,' whispered Humphrey proudly. 'Mummy, this is Rick.'

'Pleased to meet you,' said Rick politely. All the same he couldn't help being glad he hadn't met Humphrey's mother *first*.

As soon as she was properly awake, the Hag flew up to the ceiling to wake her husband. The Gliding Kilt had fallen asleep across the horns of a large, stuffed gnu. He looked rather peculiar as he began to appear, with his kilt caught on one horn and his sword, which he'd not bothered to take out because he was too tired, dangling downwards from his chest.

'Where are his legs?' whispered Rick to Humphrey.

'He hasn't got any,' said Humphrey proudly, and explained about the Battle of Otterburn.

Waking George was a problem because they were afraid he would start to scream at once and disturb the other boys in the dormitory. So they borrowed Rick's pillow and found George, who had rolled under the bed of a boy called Terence Tinn and put it over him straight away. Winifred, the sensible girl, woke by herself and came gliding down between the beds, not letting out a single wail even though she was *longing* for a wash and her bowl was being perfectly beastly.

Most of the ghosts managed to pile on to Rick's bed but the faithful Shuk had to stay on the floor with Aunt Hortensia's head because the Hag didn't approve of dogs on the blankets. Though he was getting fond of the ghosts already, the Head gave Rick a bad moment. It never looked very good before breakfast and today, with one eye gummed up and a couple of cockroaches playing hide and seek in its left ear-hole, it really wasn't very appetizing at all.

'Where's the rest of Auntie?' complained the Hag. 'Here's this nice boy going to help us—'

But at that point Hortensia's large, yellow feet appeared hovering in the air above them. She'd spent the night on a gigantic wardrobe with her phantom coach and came down grumbling that she'd got cramp in her stump.

'Right. Is that everybody?' said Rick.

The ghosts nodded.

'Humphrey has told me that you've been turned out of your home,' Rick went on.

'That's right.'

They had forgotten to whisper. Suddenly Maurice Crawler lifted his head, and let out a yell of terror. '*Things!*' he gabbled. 'Googly, ghastly *things!*'

Rick jumped out of bed and went over to him. 'Do be quiet, Maurice. You'll wake the others.'

'Stumpy Stumps,' said Maurice wildly. 'Hateful Heads. Black Bats—'

'You're bats,' said Rick sternly. 'You've been having a nightmare. Now be quiet. Close your eyes and go to sleep again.'

'Rather a *rude* boy,' said Aunt Hortensia's head, when Maurice had begun to snore once more.

'We had hoped to be able to stay here,' said the Gliding Kilt, 'but I see now that it wouldn't do. Too many children give me indigestion. Not you, of course,' he added politely to Rick.

'Well I've been thinking,' said Rick. 'It isn't just you that have been driven out of your homes.' And he explained about the whales and the cannibals and all the other things that were on his mind. 'I think you ought to find a place where *all* ghosts can live safely.'

'Somewhere *dark*,' said the Hag wistfully.

'Somewhere *damp*,' said Aunt Hortensia, rubbing some dried skin off the end of her stump.

'Somewhere with owls and bats and rats,' said Winifred, who loved animals.

'Somewhere with lots of thunderstorms,' said George.

'Somewhere with other ghosts for me to play with,' said Humphrey.

'What you need is a ghost sanctuary,' said Rick.

'What's a sanctuary?' said Humphrey.

'It's a place where people can be safe and no one bothers them. In the old days if someone was being chased by soldiers, or by anyone, and he went into a church, that was a place of sanctuary. No one could get at him there.'

'I wouldn't like a *church*,' said Winifred nervously. 'You practically *never* find ghosts in a church.'

'No, I know. I'm only explaining. I mean, they have bird sanctuaries for puffins and cormorants, where they can make nests and breed and no one is allowed to shoot them or collect their eggs. And you have them for Native Americans in America.'

'But Native Americans don't *lay* eggs,' said Humphrey.

Rick sighed. 'What I mean is, they have sanctuaries. Only they're called reservations, where the Indians can go on living the way they're used to and no one bothers them. And that's what you need. A sanctuary for ghosts.'

'A sanctuary for ghosts,' they all repeated, and nodded their heads. What Rick said made sense. It was a wonderful idea. What's more it made them feel good to think that they were looking for somewhere that all ghosts could be happy in, not just they themselves.

'I wish it could be here,' said Humphrey. He didn't at all like the idea of leaving Rick.

There was a sudden shriek from the next bed. It was the new boy, Peter. He had woken up and found himself looking straight into the Shuk's single, saucer eye.

'Go to sleep,' said Rick. 'It's just a nightmare.'

All the same, he saw that it wasn't going to be easy to explain to all the boys in the dormitory that they'd had the same nightmare. And soon now it would be properly light and Matron, who looked like a camel, would come clucking in, which could be awkward. Of course he could tell the ghosts to vanish. But telling a ghost to vanish is a bit like telling a friend to get lost. It just isn't a thing you want to do.

'Look,' he said, 'it's Sunday. I'll take you over to the gym – it won't be used today. And I'll go and see a friend of mine, someone very clever, and we'll make a plan. O.K.?'

'O.K., dear boy,' said the Gliding Kilt. 'Er, does your gymnasium have parallel bars? And a vaulting horse?'

'Yes. All those sort of things.'

'Oh, good,' said the Gliding Kilt, following Rick down the dormitory. He was not one to boast but when he was alive he had been very good at sport indeed. Tossing the caber, hurling the Clachneart and all those other clever Scottish things had been nothing to the Gliding Kilt.

Five

The friend Rick went to talk to about the ghosts was the daughter of the school cook. Her name was Barbara and she was plump with thick, long, chestnut-coloured hair, the sort of dreamy, brown eyes you get in well-fed dairy cows and a smooth, pinky-brown skin with lots of dimples. She did everything very slowly and never got excited, and if she wasn't interested in what people were saying, she just quietly fell asleep.

Although Norton Castle School was a boys' school, the Crawlers let Barbara do lessons with the boarders. This was not because the Crawlers were nice – they were exceptionally nasty. It was because Barbara's mother was a very good cook and they were afraid of losing her. Barbara never seemed to do any work, or take much notice of what the teachers were saying but whenever they asked her a question she knew the answer backwards and when there was a test she wasn't just top but so far ahead it was almost funny, like finishing half an hour early in a maths exam and getting one hundred per cent.

Rick found her in the kitchen helping her mother to make castle puddings. But she came away when she saw Rick had something on his mind and they went to talk behind an old willow tree which grew near the back entrance to the school.

It didn't take long for Rick to tell his story. Barbara didn't sneer or say he'd been dreaming but she did look very surprised. 'Ghosts,' she said. 'Who would have thought it!'

'So you see we've *got* to find them somewhere to go,' Rick said. 'Only how do we do it?'

Barbara picked a long piece of grass and began to chew the stem.

'Westminster,' she said.

'What?'

'Go to London. To the Houses of Parliament in Westminster. That's where the Government is. You'd have to go to the top for a big thing like that. To the Prime Minister.'

'Write a letter, you mean?'

'No,' said Barbara. 'Go. Take them. Keep them invisible till you get there, then insist on seeing your Member of Parliament. Everyone's allowed to see their Member of Parliament. It's a law of the land. Make him take you to the Prime Minister. Then show him the ghosts. No one will believe you otherwise.'

'Goodness.' Rick was a bit overwhelmed.

'Well you can go on messing about trying to get people to do things here but no one's got the money for a start. A ghost sanctuary would cost thousands and thousands of pounds. Only the government could *afford* it.'

'It's over two hundred miles from here to London,' said Rick. 'It's all right for the ghosts – they've got a phantom coach and anyway they can glide. But what about me? I can't *walk* that far.'

Barbara's large, peaceful forehead screwed itself up into dents and grooves.

'You'd have to do it in stages. From here till Grange-on-Trant you could go in Uncle Ted's milk lorry. That's about thirty miles. Then you could get a bus to Lonsdale – country buses are cheap. Over Saughbeck Moors you'd have to walk or hitch maybe, and then perhaps you could do the last part by train. I've got a bit of money.'

'Me too,' said Rick. 'I'll manage.'

'Do you want me to come with you? I will if you like,' said Barbara, picking two more bits of grass and starting to chew again.

Rick took the bit she gave him and thought. It would be nice to have her. Sort of calming. Then he shook his head. 'I think you'd better stay here and cover up for me. And look, see if you can get the key of the school office and be in there between seven and eight each evening. Then if I'm stuck I can ring you up.'

'Right. Do you think I could see them before you go?' said Barbara. 'I'd awfully like to.'

'Sure,' said Rick, and led the way to the gym.

The ghosts were having a marvellous time. The Gliding Kilt was hanging from the parallel bars doing a very difficult arm exercise. Aunt Hortensia had discovered the trampoline and was bouncing up and down, her nightdress ballooning over her stump, her horny feet twitching with pleasure. George was standing on his skull.

'Look at me, Rick!' shouted Humphrey the Horrible, and promptly fell off the rope.

'Goodness,' said Barbara, staring wide-eyed. 'I must say I'm impressed. What's that disgusting smell?'

The Hag, very pleased with what Barbara had said, stopped doing press-ups and came over to talk to her. 'It's wet whale liver. One of my husband's favourites,' she said shyly. 'I was wearing it when we met.'

Rick introduced Barbara and all the ghosts came down to hear what had been decided.

'A good plan,' said the Gliding Kilt, twirling the sword in his chest approvingly. 'Always go to the top if you want things done. When do we leave?'

'We thought at dawn tomorrow. That's when the milk lorry goes into town,' said Rick.

'At dawn, at dawn,' shrieked Humphrey the Horrible, excitedly, bouncing up and down like a yo-yo.

'Sooner you than me,' said Barbara as she and Rick left the gym together. 'Definitely sooner you than me.'

Neither of them noticed a tiny, black bat which had been dozing in the rafters and now flew out after them and vanished from sight. Even if they'd noticed it they couldn't have known that this particular bat was the grandson of Susie the Sucker, one of the most famous blood-sucking vampire bats in the whole of Britain. And that before night had fallen, news of Rick's march to London would have spread like wildfire across the river, through the forests of Saughbeck and on, on to the edges of the sea.

*

Rick did not exactly enjoy the journey in Uncle Ted's milk lorry.

Getting the ghosts ready had been a most exhausting job. The phantom horses were feeling frisky after their rest and didn't want to be harnessed. Aunt Hortensia, whose bunions were shooting, slapped the Shuk for dribbling on her head and this made Humphrey so furious that he refused to sit in the coach and insisted on travelling with Rick inside the milk lorry.

'I *promise* I'll stay vanished,' he said. 'I promise.'

'Even your elbow?'

'Even my elbow.'

And now it turned out that Uncle Ted wrote poetry.

> I like to see the butterflies
> I like to hear the bees
> But best of all I like to eat
> A sausage roll with peas,

he shouted above the noise of the engine. 'Did you like that?'

'Very nice,' said Rick politely, looking anxiously up at the sky. Later he learnt to make out where the ghosts were even when they weren't visible – it's a sort of knack, seeing invisible ghosts. But now he could only hope that the phantom coach was keeping up with the lorry and that everybody in it was all right.

'What about this one,' said Uncle Ted, who was obviously very proud of his poetry:

Water's Dark
Water's Deep
Some Fish Wriggle
Some Fish Sleep

'Fishes don't sleep,' whispered Humphrey in Rick's ear. 'Not properly. Because they don't have eyelids. Or eyelashes. I know because Uncle Leonard the Loathsome took us down—'

'Shh!' said Rick. He turned back to Uncle Ted. 'Have you made up a lot of poems?'

'Oh, two or three hundred,' said Uncle Ted casually. 'Hey, what's that noise?'

'George scream – I mean, your *tyres* screaming,' said Rick nervously. What *was* going on up there?

'Funny. We weren't going round a bend or anything,' said Uncle Ted.

Altogether, Rick was extremely relieved when Uncle Ted stopped the lorry and set him down just before they came to the first of the great bridges which span the River Trent.

'The bus goes right past here, you can't miss it. And give my regards to your grandmother. Hope she'll be better soon,' he said, making Rick feel terrible for a moment. Having to tell lies to people who have been kind to you is *not* pleasant.

Meanwhile, back at Norton Castle School, Barbara was knocking on the door of Mr and Mrs Crawler's study.

Mr Crawler, the headmaster, was small, and pale and weedy, and seemed to get smaller and paler and weedier with every week that passed. Mrs Crawler, on the other hand, got steadily fatter, louder and pinker-looking. The boys used to wonder whether she chewed bits off her husband while he slept.

'Come in,' she called now.

Barbara crossed the plum-coloured carpet and walked to the big double desk where the Crawlers sat. Above Mrs Crawler hung an alligator with a pleasant smile. Mr Crawler was sitting under a sad-looking water buffalo. Barbara couldn't help thinking how odd it was that you could shoot and stuff animals whereas everyone would make an awful fuss if you shot and stuffed *people* who were mostly not nearly so nice.

'Yes?' said Mrs Crawler sharply when she saw Barbara. She was not the sort of person to waste time being friendly to the daughter of the cook.

Barbara had a difficult job to do. She had to invent a reason for Rick having vanished from school and she had to make sure that the Crawlers would not ring Rick's mother to check. Rick's mother had not got any tougher since she hadn't been able to put sellotape on Rick's ears, and he worried about her. So now she said that Rick's godmother had arrived very suddenly and unexpectedly that morning. 'In a large silver grey car with the letters RR on the bonnet,' said Barbara cunningly, knowing what snobs the Crawlers were.

'A Rolls Royce,' said Mrs Crawler, impressed.

His godmother was American, Barbara went on, and only in England for a few days and she wanted to take Rick up to London and get to know him. 'It's all in the note,' she went on, holding out a piece of paper.

'Well, that seems to be in order,' said Mrs Crawler, when she'd read it. She turned to her husband. 'She asks us to choose a present for the school. Anything we like.'

'A cricket pavilion,' said Mr Crawler, who was not a modest man.

'Don't be silly, dear, we need a new dining hall far more.'

They were still arguing, getting crosser and crosser, as Barbara tiptoed quietly to the door and left. She didn't exactly *enjoy* forging notes – in fact it gave her a stomach-ache. But when people were as silly as the Crawlers there was no point in getting too upset. And really, a ghost sanctuary was so *important*.

Six

Meanwhile Rick and the ghosts were standing on the great Iron Bridge which spans the River Trent. Below them the river flowed, broad and grey and placid. Factories ran down to the water's edge; there were warehouses and smoking chimneys and barges loading coal. Bits of white scum floated on the surface of the water and there was a very strange smell.

'Delicious,' said the Hag, sniffing it up in her long, crooked nose.

Rick couldn't agree. He thought the river smelt terrible – dirty, polluted, like a great drain.

He sighed and turned to the place where he hoped the ghosts were.

'Well, we'd better plan the next—' he began, and stopped in amazement.

Something had happened to the river. In a spot just below the bridge, the calm surface of the water was broken by sudden, rearing waves, as if from nowhere, a whirlpool had sprung up. But no ordinary whirlpool because now it rose up out of the river, higher and higher. . . .

The phantom horses reared and whinnied. The Shuk whimpered in terror.

Still the whirlpool went on rising. Then, with a noise like a huge giant slapping someone, a couple of tons of water spilt through the iron rails on to the bridge where they stood.

When Rick could see again, he found that he was gazing at a most extraordinary-looking man. He had a long, grizzled beard in which a couple of dead fish hung limply; slimy, green weeds were tangled in his waist-length, grey hair, and in his hand he carried a thing like a gigantic, rusty fork.

Cautiously, Rick put out an arm. As he'd half expected, it went right through the old creature and hit the railings of the bridge.

'You're a ghost too, then?' he said.

The old man nodded. 'River spirit. Very old family, Walter's the name. Walter the Wet.' He pulled a dead fish out of his beard, made a face, and threw it on the ground. 'Stinking thing,' he grumbled.

'Are you looking for anyone?' said Rick cautiously.

'Heard some people were passing. Something about a ghost sanctuary.' He looked sharply at Rick from under his shaggy eyebrows. 'A Hag or two maybe; a Gliding Kilt . . . that kind of thing.'

'Well, they *are* here,' admitted Rick.

But by now the ghosts could stand it no longer. One by one they appeared and clustered round Walter the Wet who was sneezing a water beetle out of his nose.

'See that,' he said picking it up. 'Dead. Poisoned. Like the fish. Look at my ectoplasm.'

He stretched out a bare arm and flexed his muscles which looked pale and runny like semolina made with too much milk.

'Bad,' said Aunt Hortensia. Not to be outdone, she craned forward to show him her stump and he agreed that that was bad too.

'Three thousand years I've lived in that river,' said Walter the Wet. 'I remember the Romans going up to build Hadrian's Wall. Hundreds of them I've lured to death in that river like a proper river spirit should. I've drowned Picts and Scots. I've sent Border Raiders mad with terror, rearin' out of the water on a dark night with my wild hair flying. Loathsome I've been, an' pulpy; there wasn't nothing pulpier than me north of the Thames. But now I tell you, this river's finished.'

'What exactly's wrong with it, Mr Wet Walter?' asked Humphrey.

'What's *wrong* with it? You name it and that's what's wrong with it. Everything. Sewage. Waste muck from the cement factory. Oil from the ships. Chemicals from the fertilizer plant. Here, look at my tonsils.'

He opened his mouth, letting out a stream of dirty brown water and they all took turns peering into his throat

'Badly swollen,' said the Hag, shaking her head.

'I think there's a bit of glass sticking to the left one,' said Winifred, looking worried.

'Glass. Rusty nails. Boots. I tell you, the bottom of that river is like a rubbish dump. And dead fish – why I've gone to sleep of an evening on the river bed and woken up with a good ton of dead fish on top of me in the morning, that's as fast as they come down. Disgusting it is. Do you know what I do now when a sailor falls overboard from one of them tankers there?'

Rick and the ghosts shook their heads.

'I just go back to sleep. No need to lure '*im* to his death, I say to myself. One gulp of that river, water and 'e'll die of poisoning. That's if his throat isn't cut by an old tin can. And sure enough, by morning there he is with the fish, lying among the old bed-steads and as dead as a dodo.'

Rick was very worried by all this. In a way it was the whales and the penguins all over again. 'The poor fish,' he said.

'What about *me*?' said Walter the Wet. 'It's me I'm thinking about. I tell you, I can't go on in that river another minute. They're starting to build a tunnel under it now, to take a road through. Blinking drills rattling in your ear hole the whole night. No, it's no good, you've got to take me along to this sanctuary place.'

Everybody looked at everybody else. 'Won't you dry out on the journey?' asked Rick.

'I'll take a dip when I can,' said Walter. He gave a crafty look at Winifred's bowl and Winifred stepped back a pace. She was the kindest of girls but her bowl – if she ever caught up with it – was for washing out *her* blood stains.

Rick was frowning. If Walter the Wet was to come it meant finding the ghosts a place with a river or a lake. It looked as though this sanctuary was going to have to be rather big. He hoped the Prime Minister was a nice and understanding man. On the other hand, it wasn't much of a sanctuary if it was going to leave people *out*.

41

'I'm afraid there won't be room in the coach.' said Aunt Hortensia. 'Even if my stump could stand the damp. Which I very much doubt.'

Walter shook a puddle from his back and said: 'Going south, aren't you, to London? River flows south. So get on a boat. A coal barge, maybe.'

'A boat!' cried Humphrey the Horrible. 'Oh, I'd *like* a boat.'

'You mean drive the coach on to the boat?' enquired Aunt Hortensia.

'Could be. There's a barge goes through here about twelve o'clock carrying coal down to Porchester. The men moor by that landing stage and go for a beer to that pub on the hill. The boy can get aboard then and hide and of course there's no trouble about us.'

Walter the Wet was right. Just after twelve a long, flat coal barge came chugging up the river and stopped on the quay below the bridge. Two men were working her; a little, thin whiskery man and a big broad-shouldered man who got George very excited because he had a picture of a skull and crossbones tattooed on his forearm.

'It's me,' George kept on screaming. 'It's me; it's a picture of me!'

When the barge was safely alongside and the men had made their way to the Sailor's Arms up the hill, Rick jumped aboard, found an old sack, dug a hole in the mountain of coal and wriggled his way inside. He was just blackening his hair with coal dust so that it wouldn't show up when a voice beside him said: '*Please*, can I come in the coal with you?' – and

42

with a sigh of happiness, Humphrey the Horrible settled in beside Rick.

They all enjoyed the river journey very much. It had stopped raining, a soft wind blew across the water and the city was soon left behind. Travelling by boat is very peaceful. Cows stand and look at you, little boys wave from the bridges. Old ladies bicycle along the tow paths. Gradually Rick, though he wasn't exactly comfortable with only his eyes above the level of the coal, stopped worrying about what he would say to the Prime Minister if he ever got to him, and just looked out at the willow trees and the ducks and wondered how people could be so idiotic as to poison such a nice river with sewage and chemicals and every sort of muck.

The barge stopped for the night at Lonsdale and as soon as the men had moored and gone down to the cabin for a brew-up, Rick scrambled out. There was no point in staying on the boat any longer because the river changed course and flowed westwards after that, whereas they had to go south across Saughbeck Moors.

It was too late to hope for cars or buses – there was nothing for it except to set out on foot. They walked for one hour, then two. . . . It was a moonless night with a cold, sighing wind and Rick, who'd had nothing but a few sandwiches all day, grew very tired and very hungry. Beside him, Walter the Wet, dripping steadily, was telling him about all the sailors he'd drowned. By the time he got to number twenty-three, a Viking raider called Knut the Knout who'd fallen off his long ship right into Walter's arms, Rick's head had begun to nod. He was almost sleepwalking.

It was the kind Hag, peering out of the door of the coach above his head, who saw how tired he was and called a halt. They found a little wood in a hollow which gave some shelter from the wind. A stream ran through it, with ferns and mosses growing on its banks and a very squidgy toadstool called a Stinkhorn which made the Hag quite jealous because it smelled worse than she did.

There were plenty of sticks so Rick made a fire, taking great care not to damage the trees and then the ghosts helped him to make a bed out of a pile of leaves and he put his anorak on top of that. Of course as soon as he lay down, Humphrey the Horrible came to curl up beside him and then the Shuk lay across both their feet. Aunt Hortensia stretched out on the back seat of the coach, the Hag and the Gliding Kilt, tucking George and Winifred between them, found a mossy hollow, and Walter the Wet went to lie in the stream. It only wet half of him because it was so shallow but anything, he said, was better than being *dry*.

Rick wasn't sure what woke him up – he only knew it wasn't the ordinary sort of waking because one has slept enough. The first thing he noticed was an odd smell. Not the Stinkhorn, not the smell of burnt prunes which drifted from the Hag as she slept. No, this was a strange *musty* smell. Rats . . .? Mice . . .?

And then he saw the eyes. Weird, mad, red, greedy eyes. One pair to his left by a great beech tree, one pair straight in front of him not three yards away . . . Five pairs of eyes altogether, in a circle, surrounding him.

Cold with terror, Rick peered into the darkness. Were those fangs? Wings? Unspeakable folds of skin . . .?

And then suddenly he had it. Vampire bats. They were completely surrounded by blood-sucking vampire bats!

Seven

It was a frightful moment. Everything he'd ever read about vampires flashed through his mind: how they sucked blood from people's throats while they slept; how they robbed graves; how they lived in dark and ghastly places; how they terrorized everyone who saw them. He must have screamed without realizing it because the mad red eyes came closer. Gloating. Waiting.

And now, beside him, Humphrey stirred and sat up, rubbing the ball and chain on his ankle. Then, before Rick could stop him, he had darted forward – right at the largest of the terrible, staring eyes.

'Cousin Susie!' he shouted. 'It's me! Humphrey! Humphrey the Horrible!'

The red eyes closed, opened again, and the largest of the vampire bats came forward into the light of the dying fire. 'Good heavens! If it isn't Mabel's boy,' said Sucking Susie. She peered forward, slicing through his ectoplasm with her ghastly fangs. 'Well, you're not getting any horribler are you, my poor child.'

'I will later,' said Humphrey, sighing. He couldn't help wishing that *everybody* didn't make the same remark. 'This is Rick, Cousin Susie. He's a human and he's going to find us all a place to live.'

46

'A human, eh?' said Sucking Susie. 'Pleased to meet you.'

She edged closer. '*Very* pleased to meet you.'

Rick tried to look pleased too, but he couldn't make it. Haunting was one thing, blood-sucking was another, and as Susie came towards him it was all he could do not to move away.

'Actually, this Sanctuary's what I've come about,' Susie went on. 'I heard something from a little bat that came through yesterday.'

'Susie!' There was a shriek from the mossy hollow and the Hag swooped over, giving off stale sheep's brains, rotten eggs and dead earthworm all at once in her excitement, while she and the vampire bat started hugging each other in a tangle of black wings, noses, warts and claws.

'Well, fancy,' said the Hag again and again. 'What a pleasure, what a pleasure. How are the boys?'

The Vampire turned. 'Sozzler! Gulper! Syphoner! Fred! – Come here,' she called, and four pairs of eyes flickered and came forward into the firelight.

'Fine boys,' said the Hag. 'But thin.'

'*Thin*, Mabel? Not just thin. Skinny. Starving.' She prodded the one nearest to her in the stomach. ' "Gulper," I christened him,' she said bitterly. 'That child hasn't had a decent gulp of fresh, warm blood since the day he was born.'

'I've heard things were bad for you,' said the Gliding Kilt, coming over to join them. He could never go on sleeping when the Hag had left his side.

'Bad! They're terrible. Unbelievable. You know our valley – a nice bit of farmland it used to be. Lots of plump farmer's wives, healthy young cow-hands,

47

clean-living shepherds. Villages with butchers and bakers who slept with open windows – oh, there was lots to eat! A nip or two every other night and we vampires were as happy as you could wish.'

'You mean you used to fly in and suck people's blood at night? You really *did*?' said Rick, backing away.

'Certainly we did,' said Susie, looking crossly at Rick. 'What do you expect blood-sucking vampires to do except suck blood? The people never knew. A vampire that knows its job doesn't leave a hole bigger than a mosquito.'

'Well I think it's disgusting all the same.'

'Oh you do, do you? And what's that you're wearing on your feet, pray?' said Susie, her red eyes glinting.

'Shoes,' said Rick surprised.

'Exactly. Made of leather, no doubt. From a *cow*, I dare say. And I suppose you went up to the cow first and said: "Excuse me, Madam, but would you mind being murdered so that I can have a pair of shoes?"'

Rick flushed. He hadn't thought of it like that.

'And what did you have for breakfast before you set out. Bacon, I suppose. From a pig.'

Rick nodded.

'Precisely,' said Susie. 'What's more you didn't have the good manners just to go up to that pig and take only a little bite out of him so that he could go on living? Oh no. You had to kill the whole animal and slice it up. Really, human beings make me *tired*.'

'Rick's my *friend*,' said Humphrey the Horrible, laying his skeletal fingers lovingly on Rick's arm.

Rick took no notice. What Susie had said had

shaken him. But *could* you not wear shoes, or not eat meat? Some people were vegetarians, he knew, and maybe one could just wear gym shoes. But no roast chicken, no hot dogs, or pork chops . . .

'Well, what happened in the valley? Why did things go wrong?' asked the Hag.

'Well, first people began to drift away; they wanted jobs in the towns. Better pay. Bingo. The cinema. *More to do*, they said. Every day you'd see some family pack up and leave. Lovely, plump dinners just piling into their cars and leaving.' She sighed. 'But that isn't all. Do you know what they've done now?'

They all shook their heads.

'Flooded the whole place. Built a huge concrete dam at each end. Made a reservoir. To provide water, they say, for the factories down south.'

'Dear me,' said the Hag. 'Dear me, dear me, dear me.'

'You can say that again,' said Susie. 'There isn't a warm-blooded human left in the place. Just water and a few wretched fish.'

'You couldn't feed on the fish, I suppose?'

'We tried, Mabel, we tried,' said the vampire sadly. 'But of course fish are *cold*-blooded. We got the most ghastly chills on our stomachs. My poor old Uncle Slurper – do you remember him? – died after sucking the blood of some fiendishly cold trout last January. Gave him pneumonia. I tell you, Mabel, we can't go *on*.'

'But what would you live on, Susie, if you came with us? *There* won't be any people in this sanctuary.'

49

'Cows would do. Surely you could keep a cow or two?'

'You can't go sucking the blood of—' began Rick.

'Oh we can't, can't we?' said Susie, turning on him. 'And if you were a cow, which would you rather? A nip or two at night while you were asleep or people pounding and squeezing your udders and taking all the milk you wanted for your calf?'

Rick sighed. It seemed to be very difficult to argue with Sucking Susie.

'It isn't just me,' she said and her voice changed and became soft and motherly. 'The boys and I – we'd get along somehow. It's . . . well, look.'

She fumbled in the loose skin on her stomach and from what seemed to be a black pouch of skin she took something out and held it up to them.

'Oh!' said the Hag, and the whiskers on her long nose quivered with emotion.

It was a tiny baby vampire bat. Its little face was hardly bigger than Rick's thumbnail, its wings were so frail and thin you could see the firelight through them and as it felt the cold night air the little creature opened its pathetic mouth and made a pitiful, mewing sound.

'It's my Little One,' said Susie. 'My Baby Rose. And I don't think,' she went on, bursting into tears, 'that she's going to live.'

An hour later, the little wood was silent once again. The ghosts had gone back to sleep. Sozzler, Gulper, Syphoner and Fred were roosting in the branches of a great beech; their mother, snoring slightly, lay among its roots.

Only Rick found sleep impossible. He sat with his arms round his knees looking into the embers and thinking about the things that Sucking Susie had said.

After a while he gave a little nod and got to his feet. What he had decided to do was difficult, very difficult, but he was going to do it. He remembered reading about a man who trained fleas for a flea circus and who used to let the fleas feed from his arms. And there was a naturalist who had gone to study leeches in Africa and who used to stand in the river and let them suck his blood.

All the same, he was shivering a bit as he went over to the pile of beech leaves on which Sucking Susie lay asleep. It was all the things one heard; all those creepy stories. . . .

Susie was lying on her back, her fangs stretched to the stars. Very carefully, very slowly, Rick felt for the pouch on her stomach. Yes, there was Rose, a soft, painfully thin bundle of skin and claws. . . . He began to lift her out, stopping dead every time Susie stirred. It took a long time but at last she was free and crouching in his hand. He could feel her heart beating very fast against his fingers. 'Don't be frightened, Rose,' he whispered.

Back in the warmth of the fire he rolled up the sleeve of his jersey and placed her fangs against the blue veins in his wrist. 'Come on, Rose,' he urged her. 'Come on.'

It was an awful moment – like holding a crumb to a sick fledgling and wondering if it was strong enough to feed. Would she? Would she not?

For a moment Rose stayed still, hunched and

51

trembling. Then her head turned, her mouth groped along his arm and Rick shut his eyes as she made a sudden jab at his wrist.

And, after all, it was nothing. Susie was right. Less than a pinprick, and then he sat happily watching the tiny thing suck and feeling her warm life in his hand.

The next day they set off across the moors. No one bothered any longer to tell the vampire bats that they couldn't come. When Susie woke and found Rick had fed Rose she burst into a storm of tears. 'Oh the relief!' she cried, flying round and round Rick's head. 'Oh, you wonderful boy. I'm sorry I said all those silly things to you. Oh, my baby – look how pink her cheeks are! What excellent blood you have, you dear, *dear* boy!'

Rick had been afraid that Susie would also want him to feed Sozzler, Gulper, Syphoner and Fred and this he thought would be going too far, but she didn't. Though they were skinny the boys seemed strong enough, circling round and round the phantom coach and doing somersaults.

It was a long walk along the side of the new reservoir which looked cold and bare, not a bit like a natural lake. Walter the Wet jumped in, of course, and they could see a little whirlpool made by the top of his head moving along beside them. No one *said* anything but there was a sort of hope in the air that Walter might like to stay there. They were fond of him but all that wetness *was* trying. But when he came out he said he hadn't liked it at all. 'Clean, I grant you that. But all that concrete. Gives me the willies. No, a nice *natural* bit of water, that's what I like.'

As he walked along Rick tried not to worry but he couldn't help feeling that things were getting a bit out of hand. A river spirit meant that the sanctuary would have to have water in it; now the vampire bats needed a place to keep cows or some other warm-blooded animals to feed on. 'And anyway,' he said to Humphrey the Horrible who as usual was gliding along beside him, 'are vampires really ghosts?'

Humphrey frowned. 'I don't know. I don't think they're made of ectoplasm. I mean, you can't see through them like you can see through us, can you?'

'Still,' said Rick, 'a sanctuary's a sanctuary as I've said before. It's for keeping people safe, not for leaving anybody out. All the same . . .'

They walked all day through that gloomy valley, and as they walked the vampire bats told them of the sad things that were happening to the ghosts and werewolves and spirits all over Britain. Apparently the Hag of the Dribble, a very famous Welsh Hag who was a sort of second cousin to Humphrey's mother, had had her Dribble drained and was in a very bad way indeed.

'You don't say! Her Dribble drained,' said the Hag. 'How dreadful!'

'What's a Dribble, Mother?' said Humphrey.

'A Dribble? Well, it's a . . . well it's a Dribble. A sort of marsh, maybe. Or perhaps a bog. All I know is that a Dribble must Never Be Drained.'

There were lots more sad stories: werewolves dying of food poisoning, forest spirits having their trees cut down, ancient and famous ghosts having to haunt fish and chip shops, or discos, or Bingo Halls.

'And you'll have heard of poor Wolfram? Wolfram the Withered I mean, not that dreary uncle of his.'

'Haunting a swimming bath, I understand,' said Aunt Hortensia, who was half hanging out of the phantom coach so as to listen better.

The vampire nodded. 'He was a town ghost and when they pulled down his house they built a Public Swimming Bath instead. He says it's quite unbearable: all those dreadful pink thighs and shoulders and bottoms splashing through him all day. And of course the chlorine in the water is just *murdering* his ectoplasm.'

'Poor Wolfram. We'll have to invite him to the sanctuary as soon as we're settled,' said the Gliding Kilt, shaking his head.

Rick didn't say anything. He didn't like to point out that there wasn't a sanctuary yet and might never be one. One had to go on hoping. It was the only thing to do.

Eight

It was evening before they had crossed Saughbeck Moors and reached the place where the small road they had been walking along joined the main road to London.

At the crossroads there was a big lay-by with a garage and a restaurant from which there came one of the most satisfying smells in the world: the smell of frying chips.

'You'd better go and eat something,' said the Hag to Rick. 'You must be starving. We'll wait for you outside.'

So Rick opened the door of the restaurant and went in, blinking a bit at the bright lights and the people. It was a 'help yourself' place where you took a tray and slid it along past lots of glass cases till you got to your tea or coffee at the end. He still hadn't spent any of the money he'd brought from school and the food looked marvellous. The first thing he took was a huge plate of sausage, peas and baked beans. The sausages looked simply beautiful – sizzling hot and grilled to a turn. But then he remembered what Sucking Susie had said about cutting up pigs so he sighed and put it back and had egg and chips instead. It wasn't quite the same but by the time he'd added a bowl of tomato soup, two doughnuts and a helping of apple tart and custard, he thought that he would manage not to collapse with hunger.

And when he'd eaten and found the ghosts again, Rick climbed into the back of a parked lorry which said *Alfred Barchester. London Road. Bigglesford* and hid under a pile of sacks. There was no reason at all for doing this since the driver, who was a nice fat man called Albert with a wife and four children, would have given him a lift anyway, but Rick was too tired by then to think straight. Then Aunt Hortensia drove her coach over the top and all the other ghosts piled in just as Albert, looking rather tired, with a growth of stubble on his chin, came back to the lorry and climbed into the cab.

And they had hardly turned south, on the main road to London, before Rick – completely worn out by the day's adventures – fell fast asleep.

When he woke it was morning. Albert had parked the lorry in a lay-by and had gone to stretch his legs. They must be quite near London, Rick reckoned, because they were on a huge, six-lane motorway with a big clover-leaf flyover a few hundred yards on. Even at this early hour the traffic streamed along continuously: blue cars, beige cars, green cars, red cars; lorries and caravettes, trailers and delivery vans; huge Rolls Royces and tiny Fiats, on and on and on.

He felt in his pocket for the piece of bread that he'd saved from his supper the night before. As he lifted it to his mouth he noticed a tiny, new, red mark on his wrist. Baby Rose must have taken breakfast by herself while he was asleep. He felt very proud of her. She was obviously going to be a very intelligent vampire indeed when she got older.

When he'd finished his bread he looked out for Humphrey's elbow. It didn't seem to be anywhere on the lorry. Then he saw that there was a disused barn facing away from the road on a piece of waste ground – and there they all were: the Hag fixing Humphrey's ball and chain, Walter the Wet grumbling because Winifred wouldn't let him paddle in her bowl, Sozzler, Gulper, Syphoner and Fred looking hungrily at a cow grazing in a distant meadow . . .

But it was at quite a new figure that Rick was looking. A wavering, crazy-looking old creature wearing a monk's habit.

Not *another* one?

'I tell you I can't stand it any longer,' he was moaning. 'Look at me!' He held out his quivering, thumbless hands and Aunt Hortensia, who was the expert on ectoplasm, agreed that he looked in very poor shape.

'It's the petrol fumes and the smell of the exhaust and those idiots whizzing by all the time,' moaned the spectre. 'You've no idea what it's like nowadays. I was a monk you see. The Mad Monk of Abbotsfield they called me. Because I was walled up alive. So naturally I went mad. Ooh—' he broke off nervously. 'Who on earth is that?'

The Hag introduced Rick who shook the old wraith's rather disgusting thumbless hand politely.

'All this—' the Mad Monk went on, pointing back at the motorway and the clover-leaf packed thick with cars – 'all this used to be the grounds of an ancient Abbey, you see. I used to haunt the Old Cloisters where the monks slept. It was so lovely, so peaceful, wandering in and out, groaning and gibbering and watching the floorboards moulder where my footsteps had been. And then that wicked Henry the Eighth burnt the whole thing down.'

Aunt Hortensia's stump snorted sympathetically. 'Chop,' it said, and the Head explained that it was Henry the Eighth who had done for her also.

After the Abbey had been burnt down, the Mad Monk went on, it became a ruin and then gradually just a green field. 'I didn't mind haunting the field either. I could make the cows jump, I can tell you,' said the Mad Monk, wheezing with idiotic laughter. 'But then they built the motorway and since then it's been terrible, terrible. . . . You've no idea what it's like to have ten-ton lorries thundering through you all night. And of course the *overcrowding*!'

'There are certainly an awful lot of cars,' said Winifred.

'Oh, it's not the cars. It's the *ghosts*. Do you realize about a dozen people are killed on this motorway every week? Silly idiots overtaking in the fog or rushing along at a hundred miles an hour or sticking bumper to bumper and then piling up. And of course as soon as they're killed they start thinking this is *their* place and they want to haunt the motorway too. And absolutely ridiculous they look. I've seen ghosts glide along here in Bermuda shorts, carrying a bag of golf clubs. I ask you!'

'Poor Mad Monk,' said Humphrey, his eye sockets misting up.

Rick only sighed. He knew exactly what was coming and he was perfectly right.

'Please?' said the Mad Monk. 'Please, would you take me along? I'm very old and very mad and I so badly need a place to rest.'

'Oh well,' said Rick, 'I suppose one more won't make any difference.'

And so the Mad Monk of the Motorway came too, to see the Prime Minister of England and ask for a fair deal for the Ghosts of Britain.

Rick knew London well and he had decided that the best place for the ghosts to spend the night was in Hyde Park.

They had done the last bit of the journey in a train which turned into an Underground when it got into the centre of London. Being in a dark tunnel with slimy, blackened walls had put the ghosts in an excellent temper and everyone agreed that Rick had chosen exactly the right place.

'Nice big trees to perch on,' said Susie, swirling round the top of a clump of elms and frightening the rooks into fits. Sozzler, Gulper, Syphoner and Fred didn't say anything but they nudged each other with their wings and Rick saw them looking hungrily at a couple of tramps stretched out for sleep underneath a group of bushes. 'You won't take too much?' he begged them. 'Tramps are mostly thin and tired sort of people; they can't spare a lot of blood.'

The boys promised. Meanwhile the Hag and the Gliding Kilt were settling down in a rowing boat drawn up by the edge of the pretty lake called the

Serpentine. The Hag was smelling of wet whale liver because she thought boats were romantic and she wanted to remind the Gliding Kilt of when they were courting. George and Winifred and Humphrey were sent to sleep in a little bandstand not far away and the Mad Monk settled down in a nice, dank shrubbery behind the Gentlemen's Toilet. Walter the Wet, of course, dived straight into the Serpentine but he came up from time to time to tell them about the things he'd found, like an old armchair, a family of eels and five plastic replicas of the 1966 World Cup.

Rick was just turning to go when a small, white shape glided up to him. '*Please* can I come with you? Please, please?'

'No, Humphrey,' came the Hag's voice from the rowing boat. 'Rick's going to spend the night with a *human*. He needs a rest.'

Humphrey's eye sockets turned into bottomless pools of despair. His jaw bones trembled.

'Rose is going with him,' he said.

'I have to feed Rose,' said Rick gently, feeling the little bundle in his pocket. 'She's too young for tramps. She'd never get through their skins.'

'You get along with your brother and sister for once,' scolded the Hag. 'Listen, there's poor Winifred wailing for you now.'

On the way out of the park. Rick passed Aunt Hortensia. She was hanging in a very sloppy way in a chestnut tree, her yellow feet sticking down like a bunch of old bananas.

'You won't forget to vanish, will you?' he called out. And from under the tree, her head, lying sleepily between the Shuk's paws, said: 'Don't worry, dear child; don't worry about a thing.'

The friend Rick was going to spend the night with was called Daniel. He had been at Norton Castle School with Rick but the Crawlers made him so sick that he'd got his parents to take him away and let him go to day school. Daniel's father was a painter and his mother was a writer and they were pleasant, vague sort of people with a cheerful, pink house near the river – the kind that people were always arriving at and going away from without anyone bothering. Rick reckoned he could turn up there without a lot of questions about what he was doing alone in London in the middle of the term.

Daniel was very pleased to see him and Daniel's mother gave him some rather peculiar risotto to eat, and after that Rick phoned Barbara who was waiting as she'd promised in the deserted school office. It was nearly three days since Rick had left and she was very, very pleased to hear his voice.

'Is everything all right?'

'Mm. We've got to London. But I've kind of collected rather a lot more than I started with.'

And he told her about Walter the Wet, and the Mad Monk, and the vampire bats.

'Goodness! It's like the Pied Piper of Hamelin,' said Barbara. 'You'll need an absolutely *enormous* sanctuary.'

And then she told him what she had found out since Rick had gone.

'Now listen. Our Member of Parliament is called Clarence Wilks. Clarence Ephraim Wilks.'

'Wow!' said Rick.

'So you'd better go to the Houses of Parliament and ask if you can speak to him.'

'But nobody will ever let me *in*.'

'Rick you've got to be *firm*. Everyone's allowed to see their M.P.; I told you. That's the point of a democracy. And if he isn't at Westminster you must go and see him in his house. He lives at 397 Cadbury Avenue, Golder's Vale. It's in the North of London somewhere.'

'All right,' said Rick. 'And then I explain to Mr Wilks about the ghosts and ask him to take me to the Prime Minister.'

'That's right.'

'I've never *heard* of a boy who just got taken to the Prime Minister,' said Rick. Now that he was actually in London it all seemed much more difficult than it had done at Norton.

'There's always a first time,' said Barbara briskly.

Rick sighed. 'O.K. How are things at school?'

'All right. The Crawlers are quite happy about you being gone because your rich godmother is going to buy a smashing present for the school.'

'My rich *what*?'

'Never mind. I'll explain when you get back. Nothing's happened really. Maurice's feet are worse than ever and Masterson got detention for hoisting Matron's knickers on the flagpole. The usual stuff.'

'Well, I'd better be off.' said Rick. 'I've got to feed this vampire bat.'

'Lucky you,' said Barbara, who was a very motherly girl. 'A waste, really. I'd be better at it. More blood.'

And hung up.

Nine

The following afternoon, feeling as if a whole lot of very large butterflies were banging about in his stomach, Rick took a bus to the Houses of Parliament in Westminster. They looked very beautiful and very impressive in the sunshine, with the Clock Tower and Big Ben standing out against a clear, blue sky, pigeons roosting on the carved stonework, and glimpses behind the buildings of pleasure boats going up the Thames. It seemed perfectly ridiculous that a boy no one had ever heard of could just march into a place like that.

But of course Barbara was perfectly right. She always was. The first policeman he spoke to directed Rick to St Stephen's Gate and the policeman there showed him the entrance that visitors used, and there he was in a huge, echoing place called the Central Lobby which felt like a cross between a railway station and a church, filling in a green card which yet another policeman had given him. And when he'd filled it up and put in his own name, and the name of the person he wanted to see, a very grand man in a tail coat, wearing a golden chain took it and went off to find Mr Wilks.

While he was waiting, Rick looked round and what he saw encouraged him. There were a lot of people queuing up to see their Member of Parliament: a party of school children come to see how the government worked, two students, and a whole bus-load of grey-haired ladies – probably a Women's Institute or something like that. And as one by one their Member of Parliament came to take them inside, Rick noticed that the M.P.s all had very kind and intelligent faces. He even overheard one of them say something cheering about going to have tea.

But when Mr Clarence Wilks came, Rick's heart sank. Not that you could tell just by looking at someone but it did seem as though Norton Castle School and District had elected the only dud in the Houses of Parliament. Mr Wilks had one of those dark red, sweaty faces that looks as though it's about to explode from trying to cram too much fat in under the skin; pale glassy eyes and that superior look that people have who think that everyone who is not grown up is half-witted.

'What can I do for you, young fellow?'

Rick looked round the crowded hall. 'Could I speak to you more privately, do you think?'

'No one will hear us here,' said Mr Wilks, leading him to a slightly less packed bit of the floor. 'I'm afraid I don't have long, so make it as brief as you can. You didn't say what you wanted on your card.'

Rick swallowed. 'Well, what I want is . . . for you to take me to the Prime Minister.'

'The Prime Minister!' Mr Wilks thought this was the funniest thing he'd heard for a long time. 'The Prime *Minister*! You're a humorist. I see. Why, *I* can't get to see the Prime Minister, let alone a child!'

'It's important. Honestly.' And plucking up his courage, and ignoring the people tramping

65

backwards and forwards across the crowded lobby, Rick began to tell Mr Wilks the story of the ghosts.

'So you see,' he said when he'd finished, 'that's why I want to see the Prime Minister. Only he is *important* enough to help me set up a ghost sanctuary.'

All the time Rick had been talking, Mr Wilks had been letting out little bursts of laughter, like an over-cooked sausage spitting out hot fat.

'Ghosts!' he wheezed when Rick had finished. 'Ghosts! A ghost sanctuary! Oh, I'd love to see the Prime Minister's face if I told him that.'

'You don't believe in ghosts then?'

'Most certainly I do *not*.'

'Mr Wilks, if I could prove to you that there were such things as ghosts, *then* would you take me to the Prime Minister?'

'Oh, sure, sure,' said Mr Wilks. 'I'd take you to the moon, too. In fact it might be easier to arrange. And now if you'll excuse me – I'm a very busy man.' And still wheezing, he turned and walked away.

'So you mean it's no good?' said the Hag, her voice quivering with despair. 'He won't help us?'

Rick had got back to Hyde Park late in the afternoon. There were still people about so all the ghosts had made themselves invisible, but the pink glimmer of Humphrey's elbow, and a smell of squashed head lice had led Rick to the dark shrubbery behind the gentlemen's toilet and there they all were, waiting for him.

'He absolutely refused. He said there were no such things as ghosts.'

'Nit!' said Humphrey furiously. 'Wheezing Windbag. Festering Fool!'

'Be quiet, Humphrey,' said the Hag. All the same, the ghosts were exceedingly cast down. They had been so certain that Rick would come back with good news. Then Humphrey put his hand trustingly on Rick's arm and said: 'You've thought of something, haven't you?'

'Have you, dear boy? Is there anything we can do?' asked the Gliding Kilt.

'Yes,' said Rick. 'There is something you can do all right.'

'What?' said all the ghosts eagerly.

'HAUNT,' said Rick. 'Haunt as you've never haunted in your life! Before this evening's out, Mr Wilks is going to be very sorry he said there were no such things as ghosts.'

The house Mr Wilks lived in was called *Resthaven*. It was a large house with white bits let into the pink brickwork, like a house with measles. A long drive led up to it lined with laurels and rhododendrons. At the back there was a lawn and a summerhouse made to look like a Swiss chalet with silly, carved cuckoos on the roof, and a dog kennel which had *Buster* painted on the side. Buster himself didn't seem to be around.

Rick had chosen a good night for the haunting. The Wilks were giving a dinner party. Even in the time it took Rick to creep through the laurel bushes and make his way round to the back, a caterer's van arrived and then a wine merchant's, and inside the house he could hear Mrs Wilks shouting things to her maid.

'Now remember,' he said, when he'd joined the ghosts who were waiting in the summerhouse. 'Start off gently – just a scream or two from George, maybe the odd wail from Winifred. Then, when they get to the dining room step it up a bit. And when I give you the signal, it's full steam ahead. O.K.?'

'O.K.,' said all the ghosts happily. They were looking forward to the evening very much. It is always nice to be busy.

It was seven thirty, and in the Wilks' drawing room, which had a sage-green carpet, gold brocade curtains and very uncomfortable striped satin chairs, the dinner guests were drinking sherry and eating nuts.

All the people the Wilks had invited were Important People – the Wilks wouldn't have bothered with them if they hadn't been. There was a millionaire called Harry Holtzmann, who had got rich making guns and selling them to foreign countries so that people there could kill each other better, and a man called Professor Pringle who had written a book about What Was Wrong With Young People (which seemed to be practically everything). There was also the Honourable Lucy Lamworth whose father was a viscount, and a young man called Crispin Craig who interviewed people on television and smiled a lot. And of course there was Mr Wilks, looking hot, and Mrs Wilks who had a shrill voice and a head full of bubbly yellow curls.

It is difficult to say anything interesting while

68

waiting for dinner to be ready and feeling salty inside from too many nuts, and no one *was* saying anything interesting. They were saying things like: 'Hasn't it been hot for the time of year?' or, 'Wasn't that a truly *ghastly* film on television last night?'

And then, suddenly, there was a scream.

Actually, for George it was nothing, that scream. It was the sort of scream you might have got when torturing twenty or thirty people painfully to death, but for George it was nothing. He was just starting things off gently as Rick had told him to.

The Honourable Lucy jumped so hard that the Lamworth emeralds, crashing against her bare and scraggy chest, left bruise marks, and said: 'What on earth was that?'

The Wilks looked at each other. Then Mr Wilks got up and went out into the hall. What he saw was a young skull sitting peacefully on top of the umbrella stand. Its jawbones were open and it was just settling down for another good scream. Mr Wilks mopped his brow and went tremblingly back into the drawing room. 'It's nothing,' he said, 'the . . . er . . . the maid's dropped something. I think we'd better go in to dinner.'

Everybody filed into the dining room and the maid brought in the hors d'oeuvre. Hors d'oeuvre is always rather a slippery thing to eat: a little bit of olive, a slither of anchovy, that kind of thing – and for a while everyone was busy spearing it with forks. Then Mr Holtzmann turned to the Honourable Lucy and said: 'Do your feet feel all right?'

The Honourable Lucy, who had got wind from her anchovy, burped gently and said actually her

69

feet felt cold. Also *wet*. In fact, if she didn't know it was nonsense she would say her feet were sitting in a pool of water. Crispin Craig, who was sitting opposite, said it was odd but his feet felt just the same.

After the hors d'oeuvre came the soup. One by one the guests picked up their spoons, and one by one they put them down again.

'Does your soup taste of rotten eggs?' whispered Crispin Craig.

Mr Holtzmann said, no, dead mice.

'Mine's unwashed underwear,' said Professor Pringle, grimacing. And the Hag, invisible but working hard as she fluttered over the plates, nodded happily. It is always nice to be appreciated.

But it wasn't till the main course (pheasant in cream with potato croquettes, sprouting broccoli and red currant jelly) that Rick, hiding in the summerhouse, gave the ghosts the signal for full steam ahead. And then it all happened at once.

Through the french windows sailed Aunt Hortensia, astride one of her horses. She had borrowed some of Winifred's bloodstains to spatter her stump, her nightdress billowed out like an old, yellowing parachute and as she galloped up and down the dining room table her extremely nasty toenails clacked against the wine glasses like pistol shots.

'AAOOH!' screamed the Honourable Lucy and fell to the ground.

'A curse on the House of Wilks,' roared Aunt Hortensia's head which was sitting behind her on the backside of her horse.

'Scotland away!' yelled the Gliding Kilt,

appearing suddenly, upside down, on the chandelier.

'I'm drowning, I'm drowning!' screamed Lucy from under the table. It is not easy to lure somebody to a Watery Grave under a dining room table, but Walter the Wet was doing his best.

'Ribicus, Maerticus, Furissimus,' giggled the Mad Monk, leaping from the sideboard and fetching Mrs Wilks a wallop with his rosary. George appeared on a bowl of chocolate mousse and began to scream *properly*.

Rick judged that his time had come. He threw open the french windows and marched into the dining room.

'*Now* do you believe in ghosts?'

Mr Wilks was huddled in his chair, groaning and quivering and trying to wipe the soup off his face.

'Yes,' he moaned. 'Yes . . . yes.'

'And will you take me to the Prime Minister?'

'I can't just take you to the Prime Minister,' mumbled Mr Wilks, 'it's very difficult to arrange.'

'All right, then,' said Rick – and clicked his fingers. The next second five huge vampire bats came flying into the room, their red eyes glinting.

'Bags I that one,' said Guzzler, looking longingly at Mrs Wilks' plump, pink shoulder rising like a delicious blancmange out of her low-cut silver dress.

'No, *I* want her!' said Syphoner.

They began to squabble over Mrs Wilks who leapt on to a chair, started batting at the vampires with a table knife and fell forward, howling with terror, into a bowl of redcurrant jelly. Sucking Susie,

71

meanwhile, landed hungrily on Mr Wilks' glistening, bald head.

'Stop it!' yelled Mr Wilks. 'For heaven's sake stop! I'm being *murdered*!'

Rick made a sign to Susie and she closed her terrible mouth obediently.

'I've asked you before and I'm asking you again. Will you take me to the Prime Minister?'

'Anything,' gabbled Mr Wilks. 'I'll do anything.'

'The Prime Minister. Tomorrow,' said Rick.

'Yes,' yelled Mr Wilks. 'Tomorrow. Anything. But STOP them. STOP them!'

Rick snapped his fingers. 'Right,' he said. 'Come on everybody. We've done it. It's over.'

The ghosts didn't really want to stop, they'd been having such a lovely time. But they thought the world of Rick by now. In a second they had vanished. The pool under the table dried up, the smell disappeared; silence fell on the shattered remains of the Wilks' dinner party.

They were all in the summerhouse congratulating themselves on how well things had gone when a shrill little voice drifted out of an upstairs window.

'But I don't *want* you to go away,' said the piping little voice. 'You're a *lovely* ghost. I like you. I want you to stay with me for ever and ever.'

The ghosts looked at each other. 'Oh, dear!' said the Hag. They had sent Humphrey upstairs to haunt the bedrooms in case any of the guests went up to powder their noses and Rick remembered now that the Wilks had a little daughter.

'I did say "Boo!"' said Humphrey, gliding down

towards them shyly. 'I said "Boo!" quite a lot of times.'

But his parents were too pleased with the way things had gone to scold him for not being horrible.

'It's the Prime Minister tomorrow, then!' said the Gliding Kilt.

Rick nodded. 'It looks as though there's a real chance of a ghost sanctuary at last!'

Ten

Two days later, Rick found himself walking through the door of Number Ten Downing Street which is perhaps the most famous house in England because it is where the Prime Minister lives. Beside him walked Mr Wilks and gliding quietly above him, though Mr Wilks didn't know it, were the Craggy-ford ghosts – the Hag and the Gliding Kilt, Winifred, George, and of course Humphrey the Horrible. Rick knew better by now than to try and go anywhere without Humphrey.

The Prime Minister was in his study. He had grey hair and glasses and looked very tired. In front of him on his desk were lots of papers which he was shuffling through as they came in.

'Ah, Mr Wilks,' he said rather sadly, and Rick got the idea that perhaps he didn't like Mr Wilks all that much. 'Let me introduce my secretary. And this is Lord Bullhaven who has called to see me on . . . a personal matter.'

Rick didn't mind the secretary who was just an ordinary young man, but he thought Lord Bullhaven looked horrid. He had a sharp, white nose, small sludge-coloured eyes and black hair slicked down like sticks of liquorice.

'Now then, this is the boy with the extraordinary story,' said the Prime Minister, turning to Rick.

'Yes, sir,' said Rick.

'Something about a ghost sanctuary?'

'Yes, sir,' said Rick again. 'The ghosts of Britain – the ghosts of the whole *world* are in a very bad way. Everywhere they're being driven out of their old haunts and nobody seems to care. People build motorways over them and tunnels under them and poison their rivers.' And he began to tell the Prime Minister about his own meeting with the ghosts and the adventures they had had. The Prime Minister listened very quietly and sensibly though you could see he was surprised. But Lord Bullhaven fidgeted and twitched and sniffed in a rude and unpleasant manner.

'It's true, sir,' said Mr Wilks, when Rick had finished. 'I've seen some of them myself.'

'Would you like to meet just one family?' said Rick eagerly.

'Well, I would but—'

Rick clapped his hands. The next second the Craggyford ghosts had made themselves visible and stood respectfully in front of the Prime Minister's desk.

'Cursed be your name,' said the Gliding Kilt politely.

'Doom and Disease pursue you all your days,' said the Hag, curtseying. She was using one of her best smells, Rick noticed – crushed pig's bladder mixed with unbrushed teeth, and she was holding George's jawbones tightly between her crooked hands because she didn't think he ought to scream in Downing Street. Winifred just wailed shyly but of course Humphrey immediately came up to the

Prime Minister, laid his skeletal fingers on his knee and said: 'You *are* going to find us somewhere to live, aren't you?'

'Well,' said the Prime Minister. He was definitely looking shaken but he wasn't making a fuss like Mr Wilks' dinner guests had done. Compared to the horrible things that happen to you when you are governing Britain, seeing a few ghosts is nothing. 'Well, I shall certainly have to see what I can do. But I really don't know where—'

'Might I make a suggestion?'

It was Lord Bullhaven who had spoken. His sludgy eyes had narrowed and a muscle was twitching in his cheek. 'I have . . . an old estate on the North West Coast of Scotland. It's called Insleyfarne. The army used it as a rocket site during the war and it's been derelict since then.'

'Insleyfarne?' said the Prime Minister. 'Yes, I think I've heard of it. I'm afraid the army was a bit trigger-happy. I seem to remember the castle's in ruins?'

'That's right,' said Lord Bullhaven grimly. 'Completely bashed up. The trees are all scarred – there's not a building left with a roof on. Still, it's a very bleak place anyway – a promontory jutting out to sea. There's always a wind blowing and the land's too boggy to be any use. I don't see why you shouldn't have it for your ghosts.'

'Oh,' said the Hag, the whiskers on her nose twitching with joy, 'doesn't it sound just absolutely *lovely*, darlings!'

And Rick, as he thanked Lord Bullhaven over and over again, felt very ashamed. He'd thought he looked such a horrid, creepy man with his sleety eyes and liquorice hair and yet it was he who had brought their search to such a happy and successful end.

'Well, that's settled then,' said the Prime Minister, turning back to the pile of papers on his desk. 'My secretary will help you to work out the transport.'

As they turned to go, Rick shook Lord Bullhaven's hand again and again, and the Hag, though she usually kissed no one but her husband, kindly pecked him on his chalk-white cheek. Unfortunately, Rick could not read people's minds. If he had been able to, he would not have left the Prime Minister's house whistling so loudly and so happily that people turned to look at him in the street, and smiled.

They travelled to Insleyfarne by train. Once the Prime Minister made up his mind to do something he did it quickly. Rick had a First Class ticket and a sleeper so that he could get into his bed somewhere round Peterborough and not wake up again till they were over the Scottish border. What's more, he went to the restaurant car all by himself and ordered a huge meal: soup, and steak with fried onions and chips and grilled tomatoes, and fruit salad and cream, and ate it while the fields and hedges and cows flashed past the window. There is nothing nicer than eating on a train and Rick enjoyed himself very much. He didn't even feel guilty about eating the steak because Sucking Susie had said he needed meat to make new blood for Rose.

And while he ate he thought of what the Prime Minister had said to him just before he left.

'I'd like all this kept secret,' he said. 'If it ever came out that I'd provided a sanctuary for ghosts the whole country would think I'd gone mad. And then I wouldn't get re-elected.'

Rick didn't see it like that.

'Wouldn't people think you and Lord Bullhaven were very good and kind to give the ghosts somewhere to live, and vote for you all the more?'

'I promise you, Rick,' said the Prime Minister, 'if it got out that I believed in ghosts—'

'But you've *seen* them.'

'No one would care whether I'd seen them or not. They'd just think I was mad. If the papers got hold of it—' He shuddered.

So Rick had promised to get his ghosts to Insleyfarne without anybody noticing and they had all sworn to stay quietly in the luggage van being invisible till they got there. Even Humphrey. Both the Hag and the Gliding Kilt had given up hope that Humphrey's left elbow ever *would* vanish properly. It was like having a child with cauliflower ears or a stutter. One just had to make the best of it. On the other hand one didn't want any of the passengers noticing a pink, cobwebby thing hanging in the luggage rack now they were so near to home.

They changed trains at Inverness and the country got wilder and wilder and more and more beautiful, and then they got out at a tiny station and there was a big khaki lorry with the letters H.M.S. on the side, waiting to take them to Insleyfarne. The driver thought it very strange, taking just one boy in a huge lorry but he had his orders to say nothing and he said nothing, even when the lorry began to fill with the smell of rotting sores, even when a huge puddle appeared from absolutely nowhere. . . .

They drove steadily north. It got colder; rain began to slide in from the sea. On either side Rick saw brown peat bogs swirling with mist; granite boulders glistening with damp; trees gnarled and bent against the wind.

The road narrowed and ran along the side of a deep, black loch. And then it became a rutted track taking them across the neck of shingle and sand that joined Insleyfarne to the mainland – and there they were.

The ghosts just couldn't believe it! As soon as the driver had gone, promising to return for Rick in a few hours, they appeared one by one, clapping their hands and laughing with happiness.

'And what's more, we can stay visible for ever and ever,' shouted Humphrey. 'Can't we!'

Rick said, yes they could, and then they did a tour of their new home.

It had everything. A castle with dungeons, a derelict chapel, a ruined village with tumble-down houses. . . . Up on the hill was a burial mound and the old rocket site with some rusty Nissen huts. Every tree, every blade of grass was bent and twisted by the wind. And surrounding them on three sides, roaring and pounding and sighing as much as any ghost could wish for, was the cold, grey Atlantic Ocean.

When they had looked at everything all the ghosts went off to choose where they would like to live. The Hag and the Gliding Kilt decided on the castle.

'Oh, darlings, what a lovely, lovely home,' said the Hag, scrabbling about happily among the owl pellets and mouldy feathers that littered the old guard room.

Rick was glad she thought so. Insleyfarne Castle was a hulking black ruin. The windows – just slits, really, that people had used for pouring boiling oil through – were stuck up with the droppings of thousands of sea birds, weird fungi grew up the damp walls; evil-looking steps led downwards into dark dungeons or upwards into nowhere.

'A very nice little place indeed,' said the Gliding Kilt approvingly, shooing two large rats out of the old armoury. 'This'll do nicely for my study.'

'Can I have this room for my own, Mother?' asked Winifred, pointing to a round pit into which prisoners had once been thrown so as to starve to death. 'It's so *pretty.*'

'I'm going to sleep here,' screamed George from the top of the East Tower.

Rick left them to it and went to find Humphrey who was helping Aunt Hortensia to stable her horses.

'Very satisfactory, most delightful place, such lovely air,' she said, pushing her horses into the roofless stable through which the rain was beating down. 'I've seen the place for me – a nice little burial mound under those blasted oak trees. Nothing like dead Scotsmen for making the earth soft and comfortable. Here, give! Good dog!' And the Shuk dropped her head which she tucked under her arm and then she wandered off through the icy rain towards her tomb.

'*I* wanted that tomb,' said Humphrey, and his jaw-bones began to tremble. 'At Craggyford I *always* slept in a tomb.'

'Oh, tombs are crummy,' said Rick. 'We'll find somewhere *much* better for you.'

And they did. An old, dark, deep well which had gone dry and had a lovely soft bottom of mouldering leaves and slime. No one could see Humphrey when he was curled up at the bottom and he absolutely loved it.

'I'm Humphrey the Horrible, the Ghost of the Well,' he shrieked, gliding up and down and making his voice echo.

All the other ghosts were just as happy. The vampire bats had found a marvellous cave on the side of a cliff. It was full of seagull droppings and broken eggshells and bones from animals which had been trapped in it and died there. And it had an excellent view of the sea.

'And I've solved the food problem, my dears, simply solved it,' said Susie excitedly to Rick.

'How?'

'Seals, don't you see. Seals! The place is full of them. And they're warm-blooded animals. Mammals. Not cold and acid to the stomach like fish.' She pointed with her terrible fangs out to sea and there, sure enough, were about twenty sleek bobbing heads.

'Won't they mind—' began Rick.

'Now Rick,' said Susie reproachfully. 'How many times have I told you that we vampires know our job. And believe me the seals will like to have us around.'

'Why?'

'Because if a place is known to be haunted by vampire bats no human beings will go near it. And you know what humans have done to seals in the past.'

Rick hung his head. He remembered seeing rows of sealskin coats in the window of the furrier near his home. Even his grandmother, though she was a very nice woman, owned one.

'Will Rose be able to manage? Aren't seals rather tough?'

'Thanks to you she will,' said Susie, and her evil, bloodsucking face was soft with gratitude. 'She's so much stronger. I shall never be able to thank you enough. And I want you to know that if ever you need help, the boys and I can be with you in no time. We're usually very careful feeders as I've told you but if you *do* want anyone killed or slowly torn to death or anything, just say the word.'

'Thank you,' said Rick. He was really very touched. For a moment he thought of asking them to call on Mrs Crawler one night, but then he decided against it and just put out a hand to stroke the top of Rose's downy head where it poked out of her mother's pouch. He was going to miss her horribly.

The Mad Monk was as happy as the rest of them. He had found a small, ruined chapel – nothing more than four walls open to the sky with a mound of stones where the altar had been but it suited him beautifully. 'Oh, the quiet, oh, the peace,' he mumbled. 'I shall be able to pull myself together here. Look at my ectoplasm! It's looking healthier already, don't you think?' And he wandered off to show his muscles (which certainly looked less like cold porridge than they had done) to Aunt Hortensia.

Only Walter the Wet had been a bit doubtful. 'It's with it being sea water, you see. Salty like. I'm not used to salt water. What if I curdle?'

So they all came down to the shore to watch and very, very carefully Walter the Wet put his left big toe into the water and took it out again. Then they all crowded round and poked it and held it against the light and it seemed to be all right. So he put his whole foot into the water and when that was all right too he gave a sudden whoop and plunged into the sea.

'Smashing,' he said, surfacing. 'But tingly-like. But bracing. I feel years younger. What I reckon is,' said Walter the Wet, 'water's water when all's said and done. That's what it is. Water.' And he disappeared again beneath the waves.

When everyone was settled in they had a party. It was a celebration party because they'd found their sanctuary but also a farewell party for Rick who was going back to school in a few hours so that happiness and sadness were a bit mixed up. The Hag hadn't had much time to get things ready but she'd done wonders all the same. The old Banqueting Hall was decorated with cobwebs and the crossed thighbones of dead rats which made a delightful pattern on the slime-covered walls. Everyone had a roast toad wrapped in henbane leaves and the Hag had made an excellent drink by mixing the scum of an old water barrel with crushed Mugwort. (Rick had to do with sardine sandwiches and chocolate biscuits which the lorry driver had given him, but he didn't mind.)

Then the Gliding Kilt made a beautiful speech about Rick, calling him all sorts of things like 'brave' and 'resourceful' and 'clever' and said he thought the sanctuary should be called the Henderson Sanctuary because Henderson was Rick's second name. And he said that ghosts all over the world would come to know Rick's name and be grateful to him for the rest of eternity.

'To Richard Henderson,' said the Gliding Kilt, raising his glass of scum, and all the ghosts stood up and said: 'To Richard Henderson.'

After this everyone felt quite het up with emotion so they played games. They had Vanishing Races to see who could vanish quickest and Aunt Hortensia won which put her in an excellent mood. Then they played something called Curse as Curse Can to see who could make up the best curses and the Gliding Kilt won that. though Rick had second prize with one which began 'Cursed be the Creepy Crawlers, Cursed be their Son . . .' After that they played Hunt the Slipper only instead of a slipper they used Aunt Hortensia's Head. It was great fun but after a bit her head got so giggly that you could hear it even when it was hidden.

And then at last it was time to say good-bye to Rick. It was a bad moment for all of them but for Humphrey it was almost unbearable.

'Humphrey,' said the Hag sternly as they all clustered round Rick to see him off. 'Ghosts groan. Ghosts wail. Ghosts moan and scream and gibber. But ghosts never, *never* cry.'

It was the sort of stupid remark that even the nicest grownups make sometimes because Humphrey quite obviously and plainly wasn't just crying, he was practically floating away on his tears. 'I'll come back often and often,' promised Rick, who wasn't feeling too dry-eyed himself.

The last few moments after the lorry driver hooted down on the causeway, were just a flurry of handshakes, hugs, curses and thumps from the Shuk's three tails. Then, with a last pat of Baby Rose's head and a whiff of rotten sheep's intestines which the Hag had been keeping specially for the occasion. Rick, squeezing Humphrey's skeletal little fingers for the last time, was gone.

For the first few miles of the drive through the bleak Scottish countryside Rick's eyes were too misted up for him to see anything at all. Then, as they drove over an old stone bridge and came in sight of a small copse of hazel trees, something caught his attention.

'Would you mind stopping for a moment?'

He got out and walked over to the wood. It was as he'd thought. A wavering bit of ectoplasm which, as he spoke to it, became fully visible . . .

'Cursed be your name,' said Rick politely. 'Can I help you?'

'Cursed be yours,' said the ghost, pleased to be addressed correctly. He was a knight in armour and looked fagged to death. 'I was wondering – you don't know anything about a new sanctuary in these parts? A ghost sanctuary? I've had a dreadful time – my place has been turned into a hotel and—'

'You're on the right road,' said Rick. 'Just keep

gliding till you come to a causeway across a strip of beach and then there you are.'

'Thank you. I'm most grateful. It's a good place they tell me?'

'Not bad,' said Rick carelessly, and then he turned and went back towards the waiting lorry.

He had only gone a few steps, however, when the spook glided after him and tapped with his withered hand on Rick's shoulder.

'I've just realized who you are,' he said, raising his visor. 'You must forgive me. What a pleasure! What an honour!'

'Who am I?' said Rick. surprised.

'Why the boy who has saved the ghosts of Britain. Don't tell me I'm wrong? Surely you must be Rick the Rescuer?'

'Goodness,' said Rick, waving to the driver to show that he was coming, 'Rick the Rescuer! Well,' he said, blushing and feeling much less gloomy, 'I suppose I am!'

Eleven

Rick had been back at school for nearly three weeks. At first the Crawlers had fawned all over him and he could do nothing wrong. But as the days passed and no present arrived from Rick's rich godmother (who naturally could not send a present because she did not exist) the Crawlers went back to being their own nasty selves.

Nothing seemed to have changed while he was away. The boys still played silly tricks on Matron like putting the school hamster inside her knitting bag or pouring bubble-bath mixture in her tea and everyone went on making the same old jokes about Maurice Crawler's feet. They should have smelled the Hag's feet, Rick thought – then they'd have something to talk about.

At night, when the new boy called Peter Thorne who slept beside him, sobbed into his pillow, Rick was much nicer to him than he used to be. He really knew now what it was like to miss people so much that you just ached with wanting to see them. Peter might be homesick but Rick, he realized himself, was *ghost*sick.

'You really do miss those ghosts of yours awfully, don't you?' said Barbara when she found him sitting gloomily under a beech tree with his arms round his knees, just staring into space.

'Well, they were so *interesting*. I mean, compared to this lot.' He waved his hands at a group of boys dribbling a football and bickering about whether Smith Minor was, or was not, offside. 'And I can't help worrying a bit. Supposing seals are too tough for Baby Rose whatever Sucking Susie says. And I don't honestly think Humphrey *is* getting any Horribler. What if the new ghosts that come to the sanctuary start teasing him?'

'Oh, Rick, it'll be all right. You've done a smashing job on them.'

'I suppose so. I hate things to be *over*. You know, you have an adventure and then it's all flat.'

'How do you know it *is* over?' said Barbara. 'I've a feeling it may just be beginning.'

Rick just looked at her and shook his head. He had forgotten that Barbara was an extremely clever girl.

Meanwhile the ghosts settled down very happily at Insleyfarne. The Hag soon had the castle really nice and homelike. Jars of bottled rats' blood, and addled owl eggs, and maggot jam stood neatly on the larder shelves. She trained ivy over the gaping windows so that it made a sinister noise with its loose, tapping branches and she brought up the old torture instruments from the dungeons and hung them very prettily against the slime-green walls.

While the Hag was making the castle lovely, the Gliding Kilt planted a splendid kitchen garden. There was Henbane and Deadly Nightshade, Skullcap and Stinking Hellebore and a fine crop of turnips to make frightful lanterns out of on Halloween.

Mind you, now that they were peacefully settled in their own place, the ghosts did have time for those little, niggling worries that disappear so completely in times of danger. For example there was, as Rick had foreseen, the business of Humphrey's Horribleness. Although he was very good and went on repeating 'Every day I'm getting Horribler and Horribler,' each morning when he woke up at the bottom of his well, even a newborn baby could see that Humphrey wasn't, in fact, getting Horribler at all. His eye sockets continued to twinkle, his ectoplasm still looked like fleecy summer clouds, his ball and chain went on sparkling like a Christmas cracker.

Of course the new ghosts which kept arriving at the sanctuary didn't make things any better. They didn't mean to be rude but they'd say things like, 'Well, well!' or 'You can never tell how children will turn out these days,' – and as everybody knows, words like that can *wound*.

But on the whole, those first days at the sanctuary were wonderfully busy and happy. Baby Rose had taken marvellously to seal's blood and as she grew bigger she started following Humphrey about which helped him to feel less lonely without Rick. No one saw much of Walter the Wet who spent his time under a pile of treacherous rocks trying to lure sailors to a Salty Death Beneath the Waves which was difficult because absolutely no ships passed that way, but he came up in the evenings sometimes, splashing into the castle and telling them tall stories of what he had done. The Mad Monk felt so much better that he got quite giggly, saying Latin prayers backwards and hiccuping as he floated up and down his chapel, and Aunt Hortensia took up Art and made a collage out of driftwood and seaweed which she *said* was two werewolves eating each other up.

And of course there were the new ghosts to be settled in. Almost every day some poor, weary ghost arrived and asked for sanctuary. There were two soldiers called Ugh-tred and Grimbald who had fought with King Alfred, the one who was supposed to have burnt the cakes. They used to haunt an old, crumbling cow-byre under the Malvern hills until it was rebuilt and turned into a Factory Farm, and they had to glide up and down uttering hoarse war cries between three hundred squawking battery chickens laying eggs. They were rough, uncouth fellows, but everybody liked them. Soldiers are often very gentle and good-hearted when you get to know them.

Then there were the Ladies. Ladies kept arriving all the time. There was a Green Lady who was looking for the key to her treasure chest, and a Blue Lady who was looking for her dead husband. (She had smothered him with a pillow and forgotten where she put him.) And when they'd been at the sanctuary for about a fortnight, their old friend the Grey Lady arrived, the one that used to haunt the churchyard at Craggyford and *she*, of course, was still looking for her teeth.

Soon word of the sanctuary spread so far afield that ghosts came from other countries. Most of them fitted in very well but there was a musical ghost from Finland who was rather a trial to them. It wasn't just that she liked to play the harp on the cliff top by the light of the moon, it was that she got very offended if everybody didn't come and listen.

'Not *ghostly*, I call it, but *ghastly*,' said Aunt Hortensia crossly. She was not musical and sitting on a cliff by moonlight made her bunions shoot.

Still, on the whole the ghosts were very, very happy. Best of all they liked the evenings when they all sat in the Hag's kitchen and talked about their adventures, and about Rick.

'What was he like, this great Rick the Rescuer?' one of the new ghosts would ask.

'Oh, he had sort of big eyes and a thin face and sticking-out ears,' Humphrey would begin, and the Hag would clout him with her wings and say: 'Humphrey, what are you *saying*. Rick's ears were absolutely straight.'

Because Rick, you see, was becoming a hero in their minds and heroes don't have sticking-out ears. And they would tell and re-tell how Rick had fed the vampire bats from his own wrist and led them to the Prime Minister of Britain, and even Poldi, a rather mischievous poltergeist who had come up from Putney, would stop chucking things about and listen.

'And now here we are, thanks to him, safe and sound for ever,' the Hag would end, her whiskers twitching with emotion.

But she was wrong.

Twelve

The following morning the Hag woke with a headache. Like most mothers, the Hag often had a headache. George's screaming, for a start, frequently had her flat on her back by teatime with a damp frogskin on her forehead. But this was a much worse headache than usual. It pounded and jabbed and thumped inside her skull till she felt she just couldn't move another step. Then the backache started, creeping up her hump on one side and down the other as though someone was running a meat chopper along her spine.

'I think I'll just lie down a little,' she said to her husband.

The Gliding Kilt, usually so sympathetic, just stared at her. 'I think I'll just lie down, dear,' she repeated – and stopped because her husband had a very frightened look on his face.

'I can't hear what you're saying, Mabel,' he said. 'There's an awful buzzing in my ears and I'm so *giddy*.' His kilt was swaying as if caught in a gale and the sword in his chest had a tarnished, rusty look. But the Hag had no time to see to her husband before the most agonized screaming from the East Tower pierced her ears. It was George, of course, but this wasn't George's loud and lusty roar. This was a hoarse, pitiful scream; the scream of somebody in pain.

'Oh what is *happening* to us all?' wailed the Hag, gliding up to the tower and cradling George in her arms. His skull had gone terrifyingly fuzzy and the bones felt soft and buttery in her hand.

'What is it, darling, what is it?'

'I hurt,' screamed George. 'I hurt, I hurt, I hurt!'

Holding him lovingly in her claws and ignoring the terrible pain in her back, the Hag flew down looking for the rest of her children. She found Winifred lying on the steps leading from the dungeons. She looked completely stunned. 'My bowl's smashed, Mummy. My bowl's smashed. My *bowl* . . .'

'Something terrible is happening,' said the Hag desperately. 'We must stay together. Where's Humphrey?'

But before she could look for Humphrey, Aunt Hortensia came flying in. Her knobbly knees stuck out like ramrods; her neck stump was as stiff as a board.

'I've gone rigid, Mabel,' she said, circling the room like a great iron cross. 'Can't bend a thing. And my head's like rock.'

Everywhere in the sanctuary terrible things were happening; things which no one could explain or understand. The Mad Monk had come out in big boils – frightful red lumps, with pus oozing out of his ectoplasm and running down inside his tunic. Walter the Wet was thrown up on the sea shore, bone dry. The Shuk's lantern eye turned white and then closed up altogether so that he dropped Aunt

Hortensia's iron-hard head with a clatter and ran howling to hide under a tree.

Ughtred and Grimbald had fallen on a clump of heather and lay groaning and holding their stomachs, the Ladies slowly lost their colour: all the blue faded from the Blue Lady, the Green Lady lost her greenness; the Grey Lady became totally colourless.

'Oh, the Devil and the Dark Shades help us!' cried the Hag. 'What can it be? And where's my little boy? Where's Humphrey?'

'It's a plague,' cried Sucking Susie flying in brokenly, trailing a damaged wing. 'My boys can't fly any more, they're too weak to leave the cave. And look at my baby! Oh, look at my little Rose!'

She opened her pouch and they looked at the frail grey pathetic thing inside it in terror. Rose's little eyes were filmed over, her fangs were loose and bleeding and every so often she gave heart-rending squeals of pain.

'I don't want to alarm you,' said the Gliding Kilt, speaking with difficulty, 'but look at my right arm.'

One and all, caught by something in his voice, they turned. Below the elbow, his strong, Scottish, ectoplasmic arm was slowly disappearing into nothingness.

'It isn't me doing it,' said the Gliding Kilt in a strangled voice. 'It's being done *to* me. I can't stop it. I'm being dissolved, exterminated, *killed*.'

The Gliding Kilt's terrible words pierced the ghosts like an arrow through their hearts. The Hag wailed 'Hamish!' and threw herself against her husband's doomed body. Winifred moaned, 'Daddy,

Daddy!' A weak scream came from the melting George.

It was Humphrey who brought an explanation of the terrible things that were happening to them – a Humphrey no one would have recognized. His ectoplasm looked like an old dishcloth left in a slimy washing-up bowl for weeks on end, his eye sockets were like smudged bits of coal, and his ball and chain, as he dragged himself into the castle through the slits for pouring boiling oil, seemed too heavy for him to lift.

'Mummy, Daddy . . . everyone . . . There are some dreadful men . . . surrounding the sanctuary. Men in black coats and white collars. And they're saying awful things . . . and waving rowan branches . . . and—'

Aunt Hortensia's head gave a shriek so terrible that everyone stood as if turned to stone.

'EXORCISM! That's what it is. EXORCISM!'

'What's . . . exorcism . . . Auntie?' said Winifred, still weakly pawing the air for her vanished bowl.

'It's a way of laying ghosts. Killing them. Sending them back to where they came from. Spells, prayers, rowan berries, a thing called a pentacle . . . They use them all. Oh, my darlings,' said Aunt Hortensia, getting sentimental as people do when they think death is near, 'we're done for. We're finished!'

'But who . . . would want to . . . exorcise . . . us?' said Walter the Wet, who had dragged himself in, crackling with dryness, and now hardly had the strength to speak.

'I saw three clergymen,' whispered Humphrey. 'And a man with a pale face and black hair, egging them on. I think it was the man we saw with the Prime Minister. The man who said we could come here.'

'Lord Bullhaven!' cried the Gliding Kilt.

And in despairing horror the ghosts looked at each other as they realized what had happened.

'A trap!' said the Hag, holding her dissolving husband in her arms. 'We simply walked straight into a trap!'

Thirteen

It was true. The ghosts *had* walked into a trap – a terrible and dangerous trap. Because Lord Bullhaven was not at all what he had pretended to be. He was not a kind, rich man willing to offer the poor ill-treated ghosts of Britain a place where they could live in peace. No, he was really a very bad person and he had decided to lure as many ghosts as he could to one place and then exterminate them.

This may seem not only a cruel thing to do but also a very silly one. Even if you are not particularly *fond* of ghosts you have to admit that they don't do anybody the slightest harm. But Lord Bullhaven was the sort of person who couldn't bear anything to be even the least bit unusual or out of the ordinary. He lived in a big house in the country, called Bullhaven Hall. It was a very neat, boring house with a lot of absolutely square rooms and straight corridors. The garden was square and straight too and if a wild flower – even the prettiest wild flower like a bright blue speedwell or a golden-eyed marguerite or a scarlet poppy – dared to seed itself on one of his gravel paths, Lord Bullhaven would scream for a gardener to come at *once* and kill it with weed killer. His garden pond looked like the kind of rectangle you draw for a maths lesson and he dosed it with chlorine so that no interesting water plants should mess it up. His yew hedges all had crew cuts and even the statues were scrubbed with carbolic soap in case any moss or creeper should dare to grow on them.

Inside his house, Lord Bullhaven carried on in just the same way. He had a wife, poor Lady Bullhaven, who had married him to get away from her mama and then discovered too late that Lord Bullhaven was far, far worse, and he had two children called Wystan and Emily. Lady Bullhaven wasn't allowed to wear anything that wasn't exactly the same as what everybody else was wearing and if she tried to cook him anything like pizza or risotto or apple strudel he would spit it out and say he wasn't having any foreign muck in his house. Wystan and Emily weren't allowed to read fairy stories because they were full of weird carryings-on and they weren't sent to the village school in case they mixed with dirty, common children. Lord Bullhaven didn't like the Irish or the Welsh or the Jews or the Catholics and he loathed the Chinese, the Africans and the Greeks. He believed in flogging and hanging and his favourite saying was: *Spare the Rod and Spoil the Child*. Oh, he really was a charming man.

The reason that Lord Bullhaven had been with the Prime Minister the day that Rick came with his ghosts was because just then a country with a very nasty ruler had decided to throw out a lot of people who were living there just because they were of a different race. The Prime Minister had said they would give these people a home in England because they had absolutely nowhere else to go. This annoyed Lord Bullhaven so much that he nearly burst a blood vessel and so he went up to London to complain. The reason he didn't want these people in England was because they were *different*.

But when he saw Rick's ghosts he quite forgot what he had come for. Because however different the Chinese or the Irish or the Welsh or the Jews were, they were *nothing* to how different the Gliding Kilt was, or the Hag or Wailing Winifred or even Humphrey. Here were nasty, creepy, *unusual* things: things you couldn't spray with weed killer or torture in gin traps or just shoot. So Lord Bullhaven made this plan. He decided to offer them Insleyfarne and then when he had got a whole lot of ghosts together he would go up there and exorcise them.

Exorcising ghosts and spirits is something that has gone on for years and years. It's a way of getting rid of ghosts in a haunted house or an evil spirit that has got into somebody, and it's really a sort of magic so that it's a very stupid thing to fool about with unless you know exactly what you're doing. Ghosts that have been exorcised never appear again. They just aren't ghosts any more – they aren't *anything* any more. So really they've been killed.

To exorcise a ghost you can use all sorts of things but the best people to do it are some clergymen, sitting in a circle and saying special ghost-laying spells over and over again. Rowan berries are used too because they are bad for ghosts, and arranging sticks or stones in a five-sided shape called a pentacle helps. Some people swear by iron filings and vinegar; others believe in salt. But the clergymen are the most important and they have to be willing to go on for days on end because exorcising ghosts can be a long job.

So as soon as Lord Bullhaven had lured the ghosts into his trap he began to look for clergymen who would travel to the north of Scotland with him and help him destroy the ghosts. But here Lord Bullhaven ran into a great deal of trouble. Not as much trouble as he should have done, but trouble all the same.

Because clergymen are mostly very good, nice people who are far too busy looking after the old and sick in their parish and having choir practices and carol services and preaching sermons to want to travel all the way to the north of Scotland and sit on a cold, windy island gabbling spells over and over again and exorcising ghosts.

The first clergyman Lord Bullhaven went to see was his own vicar and he said 'No' straight away because he knew enough about Lord Bullhaven to know that he didn't want to go *anywhere* with him, let alone to the north coast of Scotland, and anyway he had the children's Sunday School outing to organize. The second vicar, who lived in a big, rambling house in the next town, said he rather *liked* ghosts and would prefer not to help get rid of them.

'But these are disgusting, unclean *spooks*!' screamed Lord Bullhaven.

But the Vicar of Netherton just smiled and said he was sorry but he wouldn't come.

It went on like this for days. Lord Bullhaven drove all over the south of England in his big, black car trying to find vicars who were willing to come with him but all of them were too busy or too sensible or too kind, and some of them thought it was shocking to go and exorcise anybody in a place of *sanctuary*.

Then in the end he found a very poor vicar who had nine children. The roof of his vicarage leaked, his church was falling down and his wife was so tired from managing on next to nothing that she used to sit down every evening after the children were in bed and cry.

'If you come with me,' said Lord Bullhaven craftily (because he was very rich as well as very bad), 'I will give you one hundred pounds.'

So Mr Wallace, which was the vicar's name, thinking of all the shoes for his children and nourishing food for his wife which he could buy, agreed to come. After that Lord Bullhaven found a very old, very deaf vicar called Mr Hoare-Croak-ington. Unfortunately Mr Hoare-Croakington (who wasn't just old and deaf but quite, quite ga-ga) thought he was being invited to Scotland to shoot grouse and this made rather a muddle later on.

The last man Lord Bullhaven got hold of was a very unpleasant character indeed. His name was Mr Heap and he had been a clergyman once but got chucked out of the church for stealing the money out of the offertory box and using it to buy whisky. But he still wore his clerical collar and called himself the Reverend Bertram Heap so Lord Bullhaven was quite taken in and thought he had got a proper vicar. Mr Heap was one of those people who look as though they were meant to be an animal – an ox or a bullock or a pig. He had huge shoulders, a red neck and a large bloated face with bristles.

After that Lord Bullhaven simply could not get

any more clergymen so the last person he took with him was a rather peculiar Professor from the University of London called Professor Brassnose who wrote books about ghost-hunting and who wanted to try out a lot of stuff like brass cymbals to bang and baking powder to sprinkle and sulphur crystals to burn, all of which he thought *might* work against ghosts but one couldn't be sure.

And on a bright day in late October, Lord Bullhaven filled the boot of his huge, black Rolls Royce with books of ghost-laying spells and folding chairs to sit on and thermos flasks to drink from while sitting on the folding chairs – and then the clergymen and Professor Brassnose got inside, and they all set off on the long drive to Insleyfarne to go and murder Rick's ghosts.

Fourteen

'I . . . don't think . . . it will be . . . much longer now,' said the Hag.

She was lying on a bed of mouldering leaves in the roofless Banqueting Hall of the castle. In her arms she held what was left of her beloved husband, the Gliding Kilt. It wasn't very much. His leg stumps had gone; his chest and arms were so faint that they seemed to be just a shimmering in the air; only the brave tartan of the kilt remained – that and his wise and comforting words.

'We've been . . . so happy together. Don't be sad.'

But the Hag was sad. She was unbearably sad. Tears rolled down her whiskery cheeks and a whole mix-up of smells: mashed mice stomachs, pig's trotters, Camembert cheese, rolled from her sick body as she remembered the wonderful times they had had together. 'And my Little Ones,' she moaned.

'It is best . . . that we should all go . . . together,' said the Gliding Kilt, whose face was beginning to break up on one side.

With her weak and aching arms, the Hag reached out to George who lay at her feet. His skull had almost melted and his screams sounded like the muffled squeaking of a mouse.

'Winifred?' whispered the Hag brokenly. A

hopeless sobbing answered her. Without her bowl, Winifred was nothing.

'Humphrey?'

No answer.

'Humphrey!' screamed the Hag again.

Still no answer. Yet just now he had been lying close beside her. Humphrey was dead then. Exorcised. Sent back for ever to where ghosts come from, never to return. Quite, quite desperate, the Hag closed her eyes and prepared for death.

Humphrey, however, was not dead. He was terribly, terribly weak and for a while, as he lay between George and Winifred feeling the stabbing pain in his poor ectoplasm, watching the pink colour drain from his tortured limbs, he just wanted the end to come quickly.

And then something happened. A little wriggling, thinking worm sat up in his brain and said: 'No. You're not just going to lie down and die. You're too young to die, Humphrey the Horrible,' said this little worm. 'You're going to *do* something. You're going to get help.'

And when the little wriggling worm in Humphrey's brain got to the word 'help' it got much bigger and reared up and said the one word: 'RICK.'

'But I *can't*,' said Humphrey weakly to the little worm. 'How can I get to Rick? I can't even move.'

'Can't you?' said the wriggling worm. 'Are you sure you can't? Try. Move one leg. Go on – try. There. Now the other.'

'It *hurts*,' said Humphrey to the little worm.

'That doesn't matter. Now up. Glide. Go on. Go *on*.'

And then Humphrey really was up in the air and gliding, weakly and slowly but gliding . . . past Aunt Hortensia lying like an iron girder on her tomb, past the poor Shuk whimpering in agony with only one tail left of his three, past the moaning, fast-dissolving Ladies . . .

As he came over the causeway which separated Insleyfarne from the mainland, he felt a stab of pain so agonizing that he nearly fell to the ground. He was flying right into the beam of Mr Wallace's exorcism. Mr Wallace was the youngest and the strongest of the clergymen. He was also the nicest, and though he hated the job he was doing he thought it only fair to do it well. So he was sitting on Lord Bullhaven's folding chair waving a rowan wand in one hand and gabbling Spell 293 out of the ghost-laying book as hard as he could.

> Creeping Nasty Crawling Creatures
> Ghosts With Hideous Monster Features
> Go We Tell You, Leave This Spot
> Go Into The Grave And Rot . . .

There was a lot more of this spell and if Mr Wallace had been able to get to the end of it, Humphrey would probably have been done for. But poor Mr Wallace only had a very thin and threadbare coat and it was bitterly cold sitting on the shingle with the wind howling in from the sea and quite suddenly he was attacked by a terrible fit of sneezing.

It lasted only a few moments, this gap in the exorcism, but it was enough. Humphrey was able to glide on over Mr Wallace's head and to set off on his long and exhausting journey to find Rick the Rescuer.

It was a journey that Humphrey never forgot. Though he grew a little stronger as he got away from the exorcism, he was still very weak. His ball and chain felt like a ton of lead, and sometimes he was so dizzy he didn't know whether he was gliding on his head or his heels. Worst of all, he wasn't too certain of the way he had to go. South East, he knew, but exactly how far? What if he should miss Rick's school altogether?

But he couldn't; he *couldn't* miss it. His parents were dying; George and Winifred, and all the other ghosts who had been trapped so cruelly and hideously on Insleyfarne . . . He *had* to find Rick. What Rick could do to save an island full of dead and dying ghosts, Humphrey never thought. He wasn't very clever. He just had faith.

It had been a clear and blustery morning when he set out from Insleyfarne. Now the clouds gathered; it began to rain and the wind was dead against him. Without the protection of the phantom coach he was bitterly cold and he was shivering so much that he began to lose height.

'I can't do it,' he sobbed. 'I can't go all that way.'

Then he remembered what the Gliding Kilt had told him once. 'If you've got something difficult to do, don't think of it all laid out in front of you. Just think of the one next step. You can always take just one step more.'

So Humphrey glided one step more and then

another and another, and at last the land below him changed and became gentler: fields and hedges instead of wild moorland, and he knew he was getting to the English border. East now . . . over the river, and a moment of panic as a flock of starlings rose suddenly into the air and nearly blinded him. And then, wasn't that a familiar fir wood and there, in the clearing . . . Was it . . .? Oh it had to be . . . Yes! There they were! As smelly as ever, hung out on the window sill by the other boys – Maurice Crawler's striped and disgusting football socks!

With a sob of exhaustion, Humphrey lost height, glided through the dormitory window and fell, in a heap of utter weariness, on to Rick's bed.

Rick was in Classroom V having a history lesson. The lesson was about Henry VIII whom Rick had never liked anyway and now really hated for having cut off Aunt Hortensia's head and burnt down the Mad Monk's monastery and making such a nuisance of himself generally.

Barbara, sitting beside him, looked as though she was asleep but Rick knew that if Mr Horner asked one of his silly, pointless questions, she would know the answer straight away.

'Please, sir, can I be excused?' said Maurice Crawler.

Rick exchanged a glance with Peter Thorne who sat on his other side. All the boys knew what Maurice did when he was excused. He went up to the dormitory, took a box of sweets from under his pillow and stuffed himself before he came back to the classroom. Probably Mr Horner knew it too but what could he do with Mrs Crawler always defending her 'Honeybunch'.

'Very well,' said Mr Horner, and started telling the class about Henry's second wife, poor Anne Boleyn.

He hadn't got very far before the classroom door burst open and Maurice came tottering in, trembling like a great, white jellyfish.

'A THING!' He pointed at Rick. 'Like before. On Henderson's bed. A b . . . beastly, ghastly g . . . ghost!'

'Now really, Crawler,' began Mr Horner. And then: 'Henderson! How dare you leave the class-room without—'

But Rick, with Barbara running at his heels, had gone.

'Humphrey! Oh, Humphrey!' Rick swallowed the lump in his throat. 'What's *happened*? What have they *done* to you?'

'I'm all right,' said Humphrey weakly, waving a skeletal finger. 'It's all the others . . . Rick, it was a trap. And they're all dying. Perhaps dead. My mother and father, George, Winifred – *everybody*!'

And between the hiccuping sobs which shook him now that he'd reached Rick at last, he told him of the dreadful things that were happening at Insleyfarne.

'You've *got* to help us, Rick,' said Humphrey. 'And *quickly*, before—'

He broke off as the door of the dormitory burst open and Peter Thorne rushed in.

'They're all coming up, Rick – Mr Horner and the Crawlers and beastly Maurice – to see this—' He

108

stopped dead. 'Goodness! It's true then. It really *is* a ghost.'

'Yes, it's a ghost,' said Rick quietly. 'It's also my friend and he needs help. Try and stop them coming in.'

Without any more fuss, Peter rushed back to the door and started pulling a chest of drawers across it. For someone so frail-looking he was surprisingly strong.

'Humphrey, can you still vanish or are you too weak?'

Humphrey turned his grey, exhausted face to Rick's. 'I'll ... try ...' he said. It was obviously a tremendous effort but after a moment his poor, lumpy ectoplasm began to disappear and only his elbow hung like a shred of old sheep's wool in the air.

The hammering on the door began. Rick ignored it. His face had gone as grim as stone. As soon as Humphrey had said the dread word 'EXORCISM' he knew how serious the danger was.

'How many clergymen were there?'

'Three,' came Humphrey's voice. 'And another man with a beard. And Lord Bullhaven, of course.'

Rick wasn't a silly, daydreaming kid. To tackle five grown men he'd need help.

'Open up,' screeched Mrs Crawler outside the door. 'Open up, you wicked children.'

'I can't hold them much longer,' said Peter, braced against the chest of drawers. And suddenly Rick remembered something. Peter was tiny and pale and thin with fair curls and pansy blue eyes. What's more, he'd been so homesick the first few weeks of

109

term that he'd practically never stopped crying. And yet no one teased or bullied him. Not that they hadn't tried. Right at the beginning, Maurice Crawler had tried shoving him against the rough-cast corridor leading to the gym – and then suddenly Maurice was sprawling on the floor.

'Was it Judo?' Rick had asked Peter, because Maurice was at least twice as big.

Peter had shaken his head. He used Judo quite a lot, too, he said, but this was something called Aikido. Japanese, too, but reckoned to be neater. His father had taught him. And then when he got to the word 'father' he started snivelling again and Rick had left him. Now, though, he made up his mind.

'You'd better come with us,' said Rick to Peter, pushing open the dormitory window. 'Can you get down the ivy, Barbara?'

Barbara nodded. She was so furious at what they'd done to Humphrey that she couldn't even speak.

'Come on, then,' said Rick. And as they climbed down the ivy and started running down the grav-elled drive away from school, he turned to comfort Humphrey. 'It's going to be all right,' said Rick the Rescuer. 'I promise you, it's going to be all right.'

Rick spoke bravely but he wasn't nearly as sure or as hopeful as he sounded. Insleyfarne was over three hundred miles to the North West – ghosts glide so fast they can get you very muddled about dis-tances. Even if they could find a car or train to take them there it would most likely be too late. 'It's how to get there *quickly*,' said Rick, thinking aloud.

He had forgotten Barbara.

'I know how,' she panted, running beside him. 'Miss Thistlethwaite, that's how. It's Miss . . . This- tlethwaite we need.'

Rick was so surprised, he stopped dead. 'Miss Thistlethwaite? Are you crazy?'

Miss Thistlethwaite was the visiting music teacher. She taught the violin and the piano, arriving on her bicycle on Thursday mornings and Tuesday afternoons. She was a rather odd-looking lady who wore long, flowing black dresses hitched up with dressing-gown cord and could be heard screaming in pain when Maurice Crawler missed his Top E or Smith Minor crashed like a runaway tank through Schubert's *Cradle Song*.

'Let's see, it's a full moon tonight, isn't it?' said Barbara. 'Yes. Then it's the village we want.'

If it had been anyone but Barbara, Rick would have argued. Now he just shrugged and set a steady pace, looking backward now and then for signs of the Crawlers.

The village hall was a low, wooden building in a lane beside the church. The door was locked, the blinds were drawn. A notice painted in red said *Norton Women's Tea Club. Members Only.*

'Try the back.'

At the back of the hall was a little door leading into a small cloakroom. Quickly the children crept inside, and the worn scrap of grey that was Hum- phrey's elbow followed. Then they opened the door into the hall a crack and peered through.

The hall was dark except for the light of tall candles set in branched candlesticks on the window sills, and a strange, blue flame flickering in a bowl of

111

charcoal on the upright piano. Three sides of the room were lined with trestle tables on which were all the usual things one brings, or buys, at village sales: jars of jam, and cakes, and crochet mats. . . . But the thirteen ladies who seemed to make up the Norton Tea Club were not, at the moment, buying or selling anything.

No, they were dancing. A kind of chain dance, weaving in and out, kicking up their legs and stamping. . . .

'Look at their hats,' whispered Barbara.

And indeed the ladies' hats *were* strange. Their own Miss Thistlethwaite wore a hat decorated with yew berries, mistletoe and poppies. Mrs Bell-Lowington, who lived in the manor, had a whole stuffed owl on her head. Miss Ponsonby, who ran the post office, wore a pink cloche embroidered with black triangles.

And now they had joined hands and were singing. The tune was pretty but the words were odd.

Eko; Eko Azarak! Eko; Eko Zomelak!
Eko; Eko Cernunnos! Eko; Eko; Arada!

sang the ladies of the Norton Village Tea Club.

'Ready?' whispered Barbara – and opened the door.

The circle of ladies stopped dead still. Their mouths shut on the last word of their song and thirteen pairs of eyes with rather unpleasant expressions fixed themselves on the three children.

'Miss Thistlethwaite?' said Barbara. 'Please, Miss Thistlethwaite?'

Miss Thistlethwaite took an uncertain step forward.

'Fredegonda,' thundered Mrs Bell-Lowington, who had been leading the dance, 'what are these children doing here?'

Miss Thistlethwaite shook her head. 'I don't know, Nocticula,' she said nervously.

'Oh *please* don't be cross,' cried Barbara. 'We know you're witches and we won't tell a soul. Only, please, *please* can you help us? We're in trouble!'

A flutter passed through the coven of witches, the circle broke, and Fredegonda (which was Miss Thistlethwaite's witch name because it is difficult to be a witch with a Christian name like Ethel) came towards them, followed by the chief witch, Nocticula. (Her Christian name was Daisy which was even worse.)

'What is it that you want of us?'

For answer, Rick clicked his fingers and poor Humphrey, shivering with exhaustion, appeared before the witches. For a moment they looked in silence at his lumpy, curdled ectoplasm, his swollen ankles, the rash round his battered face. . . .

'Exorcism!' thundered Nocticula. 'A disgusting habit.'

'The poor little fellow,' said Fredegonda.

'That's the iron-filings spell, I think,' said Melusina, who was really Miss Ponsonby from the post office, lifting Humphrey's left hand. 'A very cruel and uncivilized spell, I always think. Look at the softening of the joints.'

'Who was responsible for this?' said Nocticula her eyes glinting. Witches and ghosts have always been fond of each other and the sight of Humphrey made her very angry.

So Rick told them the whole story: of the ghost sanctuary and the trap it had proved to be; of the dreadful plight of the ghosts on Insleyfarne; of their desperate need to get up there *at once*.

'On a broomstick maybe?' said Peter who was rather young.

'A broomstick!' snarled Nocticula.

'Or whatever you use nowadays? A vacuum cleaner?' said Peter.

'You may be young,' said Nocticula, 'but there is no reason to be silly. I doubt if witches ever flew on broomsticks. They certainly don't do so now.'

'But isn't there any way you can get us there?'

'Witchcraft isn't a lot of stupid tricks,' said Nocticula. 'Witchcraft is about *power. Willpower. Making things happen.* White witches make good things happen. Black witches make bad things happen. Flying about on broomsticks, turning people into toads – that's all cheap trickery and rubbish.'

'So you can't help us?' said Rick sadly.

'I don't remember saying that,' said Nocticula irritably. 'In fact I *didn't* say it.' She turned to the other witches. 'Come on, girls, quickly now.'

Rick and Peter and Barbara followed the witches over to the trestle tables lined against the wall. Now that they were close up to them they could see that some of the exhibits were rather odd. In the *Cookery* section there were jars of wormwood jam, bottles of powdered gall and a lot of small jars labelled CORIANDER SPELL or PERIWINKLE SPELL or LOVE PHILTRE: *Dilute as needed.*

114

On the table labelled *Needlework* there were little sachets filled with Moonwort and Cinquefoil and Smallage and in the *Pottery* part were cauldrons and double-handled cups with strange signs painted round the sides.

But the table where Nocticula now stopped was the most interesting of all. It was covered in hand-made puppets – beautiful life-like puppets in modern clothes.

'Oh look, there's Mrs Crawler,' said Rick suddenly, pointing at a fat puppet in a blue dress which had won second prize.

'And there's the Vicar!' said Peter.

'And Ted – the groundsman.'

As they looked carefully the children realized that every one of the puppets looked exactly like somebody who lived in, or around the village.

'This one, I think,' said Nocticula. She picked up a puppet in a dark blue flying suit and earphones.

Rick recognized it at once. It was a young man called Peregrine Rowbotham who lived in Rowbotham Hall about three miles north of the village. His father was very rich so all Peregrine did was to go to lots and lots of parties and fly about in his private Piper Cherokee aeroplane.

'Right,' said Nocticula. She hitched up her skirt, fished a piece of chalk out of the pocket of her green, Chilprufe knickers and drew a triangle on the floor. Meanwhile Fredegonda threw some incense on to the bowl of glowing charcoal and Melusina went over to the *Cookery* table and began pounding up various powders on a wooden board. It was rather like watching nurses get ready for an operation.

115

'We're out of Graveyard Dust,' said Melusina.

'Not important,' said Nocticula impatiently. 'Use Dragon's Blood.'

When the preparations were over, they put the puppet down in the middle of the triangle and stood round it. You could see that they were all concentrating very hard.

'In the name of Cernunnos the Horned One, we wake thee from sleep, O Peregrine Rowbotham,' said Nocticula.

'May the travel thirst roam through your limbs and make you rise from your bed,' chanted a second witch.

'May your soul seek greedily the distant soil of Insleyfarne,' said a third.

'Wake, O Peregrine! Wake, wake, wake and come!' cried all the witches.

Then Nocticula took a hatpin out of her hat and stuck it gently into the puppet's foot. The witches raised their arms and a blue flame shot upwards from the crucible.

> Hear My Will; Attend To Me
> As I Will So Mote It Be!

cried all the witches.

Then: 'Unlock the door,' ordered Nocticula.

Two minutes passed, five, ten. . . . And then they heard the sound of a car screeching to a halt outside. There was a knock on the door. It creaked open and on the threshold, blinking and looking totally bewildered, stood Peregrine Rowbotham.

'I say, would anyone like a jolly old spin in my

116

crate up to Insleyfarne?' he said. 'I suddenly had a fancy to see the place.'

And with their mouths hanging open, Rick and Barbara and Peter went slowly up to him and said, 'Yes, we would. Please.'

Fifteen

Poor Peregrine Rowbotham had been lying in his four-poster bed in Rowbotham Hall, wearing his best blue silk pyjamas and snoring gently. It was the middle of the afternoon and an odd time to be asleep but Peregrine had been to a party which had gone on all night and hadn't got to bed till eight in the morning.

At first Peregrine's dreams were the sort he usually had: about beautiful girls and fast cars, and the horses he had backed winning their race. And then gradually his dreams changed. He saw purple heather and brown, tumbling streams and bracken; and then a promontory of land stretching out into the wild, Atlantic sea. It was a bleak and windblown place, with stunted trees and a dark, ruined castle but Peregrine, in his dream, wanted to go there more than anything in the world.

'Insleyfarne,' said Peregrine, talking in his sleep, 'I want to go to Insleyfarne!'

A sudden, jabbing attack of cramp in his right leg jerked him awake. Without quite knowing what he was doing, he began to pull on his clothes. . . .

'Insleyfarne,' he went on saying, standing there in his underpants. 'Insleyfarne.'

But when he was dressed and had climbed into his gleaming E-type Jag, he found he didn't want to drive straight to the field where he kept his aeroplane. Something was making him turn left instead of right, towards the village.

'Lonely,' said Peregrine, still in that dazed voice. 'Poor Peregrine needs *friends* to go to Insleyfarne.' And he had driven straight to the village hall.

And now he was flying steadily north with three unknown children in the plane beside him and an odd, cobwebby scrap of grey that kept catching his eye when he turned round.

'It was hypnotism, really, wasn't it?' said Barbara.

Rick shrugged. 'Hypnotism. Willpower. Witchcraft – it's all the same I guess. Just as long as we're not too *late*.'

They flew over dark lochs and rocky islands, over spruce forests and rolling moors. The country grew wilder, bleaker. And then at last:

'Insleyfarne!' cried Rick. 'Look! There!' And Peregrine banked, circled and came neatly in to land on a long, empty beach of hard, packed sand to the north of the promontory.

It is not easy to surround what is practically an island, and quite a big one, with only four men, but Lord Bullhaven had done his best.

He'd put Mr Heap, the clergyman who looked like a pig, on a rocky outcrop just below the castle, and Mr Wallace, the nice one with nine children, on a shingle beach near the causeway which led to the mainland. Dotty Mr Hoare-Croakington was up on the hill by the rocket site and Professor Brassnose was down by the ruined chapel and the well. All of them had folding chairs to sit on and packets of sandwiches to eat and thermos flasks of hot coffee to drink, so that they could go on and on exorcising and of course all of them had books of ghost-laying spells and rowan twigs, and Professor Brassnose also had bottles of vinegar and iron filings and cymbals to bang and a hold-all of strange ointments and powders from his laboratory.

Lord Bullhaven himself was too mad to sit quietly on a chair exorcising. He just rampaged round the island yelling things like, 'Vile, disgusting creepie-crawlies!', 'Filthy, foul scum!', 'Britain for the British', and making lopsided pentacles out of anything he could lay his hands on. And if any of the clergymen stopped even for a second, just to stretch his legs, Lord Bullhaven came charging up and said: 'Back, blast you! Back to your post.'

Mr Heap didn't take much notice of the aeroplane that passed overhead and landed a mile or two to the north. He was sitting with his back to the sea and his big, bristly face turned up to the castle. Cigarette packets and sandwich papers flapped round his ankles because he was a litter lout as well as a crook and he was gabbling ghost-laying spell No. 976 with such venom that bits of spittle came out of his mouth and dropped disgustingly on to the pages of the book.

> Spider, Scorpion, Ugly Toad
> Follow on your Hellbound Road,
> Bile and Blisters, Blasts and Plague
> Every Sore and Ill and Ague!
> Out with Hag and Vampire Bairn
> Let the Earth Be Clean Again,

gabbled Mr Heap.

And then quite suddenly he wasn't sitting on his chair. He was sitting on a patch of wet and slippery rock and a small, fair boy who seemed to have come out of the sea was standing over him.

'I'd like you to stop now, please,' said Peter Thorne politely.

'Why . . . you . . . you. . . .' Mr Heap struggled to his feet and put out a huge hairy hand to seize Peter by the throat.

Only it wasn't any longer Peter's throat. It was just thin air and Peter himself had somehow become a ball of lead charging straight at Mr Heap's fat and unprotected stomach.

'Yaaow!' yelled Mr Heap and crashed down on to the rocks again. By the time he was up once more, Peter was running up the steps of the castle, the book of ghost-laying spells under his arm.

'Give me back that book, you little swine,' yelled Mr Heap.

Peter turned at the top of the steps. 'If you want it, come and get it,' he shouted.

He ran on up the steep cliff track to the draw-bridge which crossed the pit of slime and mud that was the castle moat. Then he stopped quietly and waited for Mr Heap – steaming with sweat and gibbering with fury – to catch up with him.

'Here's your book,' said Peter sweetly.

Mr Heap lunged forward to grab it. Peter narrowed his eyes, concentrating very hard. The Uki-Otoshi hold was a bit tricky; one had to get it exactly right. Then he dropped on one knee, stiffened his other leg – and as the flabby, panting man collapsed against him, pushed with all his might.

And Mr Heap sailed quietly into the air and fell – all sixteen quivering stone of him – with a splash that sent up a flock of startled seagulls – into the green and putrid waters of the moat.

Meanwhile poor Mr Hoare-Croakington, up on the bleak and windy hill by the rocket site, was getting more and more confused. He had been so absolutely *certain* that he had been asked to Insleyfarne to shoot grouse. Mr Hoare-Croakington had never before shot grouse – he had never before shot *anything* – and he wanted to very much.

But no one had handed him a nice shotgun and some pretty, pink cartridges. Instead they had put him on a canvas chair on a very cold hill and told him to say poetry out of a book. Mr Hoare-Croakington was not fond of poetry and he found the whole thing very disappointing and sad.

After a while however he cheered up and the reason was this: at the hotel where they had spent the night, Lord Bullhaven had ordered everyone's thermos flask to be filled with coffee so as to keep them awake. But the hotel kitchen-maid, who was very overworked, had made a mistake and mixed up Mr Hoare-Croakkigton's flask with the flask of someone called General Arkwheeler who always ordered *his* thermos to be filled with neat whisky.

So every time Mr Hoare-Croakington took a little sip, things got more and more cheerful and more and more muddled up.

Curse (hic) and Plague (hic) and Bell and Book
Drive away (hic, hic) this ghostly Spook,

sang Mr Hoare-Croakington. And then: 'Bang, bang,' he said. And again: 'BANG!'

'No,' said Barbara, appearing quite suddenly out of the waist-high bracken.

'No?' said Mr Hoare-Croakington, very surprised to see her. 'No bang-bang?'

Barbara shook her head. 'Well, there's nothing to bang bang, is there?' she pointed out, gently easing the ghost-laying book off the old man's knees.

'Grouse?' said Mr Hoare-Croakington hopefully.

'No grouse here,' said Barbara firmly, scuffing Mr Hoare-Croakington's rather grotty pentacle aside with her shoe. 'But I know where there are some lovely, lovely grouse. If you come with me. Big, FAT grouse with huge plump chests. . . .'

Mr Hoare-Croakington liked the sound of that.

'Huge, plump chests. . . .' he murmured happily.

And very quietly and meekly he let Barbara lead him away by the ends of his woollen muffler towards Lord Bullhaven's big, black car which was parked on the far side of the causeway.

Rick wasn't normally much of a boy for fighting. He preferred to think things out. But on his way to tackle Professor Brassnose, he passed the ruined chapel. And when he'd seen what was inside – the Mad Monk writhing in agony on a sea of pus made from his own boils – Rick wasn't interested any longer in *thought*.

Professor Brassnose was sitting on his chair beside

the well, clashing his brass cymbals together and gabbling a spell from the book on his knees. A bottle of iron filings and vinegar was propped against his chair and the rest of his ghost-laying paraphernalia spilled out of a big carpetbag nearby.

At least that was how it was one minute. The next minute the contents of the hold-all were scattered to the winds, the ghost-laying book had been snatched from his hands and the pages ripped to shreds, and the bottle of vinegar and iron filings lay smashed to pieces against a stone.

'Stop it,' squeaked Professor Brassnose, waving his arms. 'Stop it at—'

'Don't you dare to speak to me, you filthy, murdering swine,' said Rick managing to kick the Professor's chair, his shins and his stone pentacle all at once.

'Help!' screamed the Professor, who was definitely not a fighting man. 'Lord Bullhaven! Help! Help! There's a bad moy down here. I mean a mad boy. Help! Help!'

Lord Bullhaven was in an evil mood. He had just come across a green, slime-covered cursing THING which turned out to be Mr Heap, stumbling towards the car and refusing absolutely to return to his post. Then he had gone up to the rocket site and found Mr Hoare-Croakington's chair empty. And now that idiot, Brassnose. . . .

'Coming,' shouted Lord Bullhaven and started lumbering downhill towards the chapel, slashing about with his rowan switch as he came. When he saw Rick his sludge coloured eyes widened like dustbin lids. 'You!' he thundered.

124

Rick stood still and faced him. 'Yes,' he said. 'Me. The boy to whom you promised *sanctuary* for his ghosts.'

Lord Bullhaven's face had turned purple. 'Get off my land,' he screamed. 'Get off it and stay off it.'

For answer, Rick pulled over Professor Brassnose's chair, tipping the squealing Professor out on to the grass and hurled the cymbals into the well.

Lord Bullhaven now seemed to lose the last scrap of his reason. He ran at Rick and started hitting him viciously with his rowan stick. 'It's your fault, you young devil, you've spoilt my plans. I'm going to kill you. I'm going to—'

'No,' said a quiet voice, 'I think not.' It was Mr Wallace, the nice clergyman with the nine children, who had heard the shouting and come to see what was up. 'You're hurting the boy,' Mr Wallace went on, still in a quiet, level voice. 'Let him go.'

Lord Bullhaven gave Rick a last blow across the shoulders and turned on Mr Wallace. 'You're on their side,' he screamed. 'You're in with the spooks. You're a paid agent, you're a witch lover. I'll have you flogged if you don't go back, I'll have you hanged—'

He put down his head, ready to charge at Mr Wallace. Mr Wallace, who had been Boxing Champion at his Theological College, just had time to ask God, very quickly, to forgive him. Then he bunched up his fists – and that was that.

*

They were dragging the unconscious Lord Bullhaven towards the car, when the most dreadful, desolate and shuddering scream came from the castle.

Rick turned white and began to shiver. 'It's the Hag,' he said, 'I recognize her voice.'

'You go and see to them,' said kind Mr Wallace, to whom Rick had told the whole story. 'I'll drive this lot back to the hotel.'

Rick nodded his thanks. Then with Barbara and Peter at his heels, he turned and ran towards the castle.

Sixteen

'Oh, *Hag*,' cried Rick, and it was all he could do not to burst into tears then and there. She was only just there still; her whiskery nose had gone and her crooked back, and her scaly black wings were as weak and worn through as winter leaves. But what frightened Rick most of all was that she was giving off absolutely no smell.

'Rick!' whispered the Hag, looking pitifully up at him.

'It's all right, we've got the men who were exorcising you. It's over!' cried Rick, bending over her.

The Hag tried to shake her head. 'Too late,' she murmured brokenly. 'Look!'

She put out a faint claw and pointed to a piece of tartan cloth spread on the floor beside her. It was absolutely all that was left of the Gliding Kilt. On the other side of the wretched Hag was a little pile of yellowish bubbles – George's softened and melted skull. Winifred, wrapped in her shroud, had fainted.

'And my Little One . . . lost for ever. My Humphrey. He's been laid!'

'No, Mother! No, I haven't. Look at me!' said Humphrey. As soon as the exorcism stopped he'd felt his strength return and left the aeroplane. Now as he glided up to hug his mother, he looked almost his old self.

'I went and fetched Rick and he got the people who were trying to lay us. He went bang wallop, wallop bang,' said Humphrey, waving his arms excitedly. 'And Peter and Barbara. I knew Rick would rescue us.'

'*Humphrey*,' said the Hag. She couldn't believe that it was really him and kept passing her claws through and through his ectoplasm to make sure she wasn't dreaming.

Suddenly she made faint, flapping movements with her wings, like a stranded chicken, and they realized she was trying to sit up.

'We must . . . help the others,' said the Hag. 'If the exorcism's over perhaps there is still hope for them. We must get organized.'

'A hospital?' Barbara suggested.

The Hag nodded. 'Bring . . . everyone . . . in here.'

So Rick and Barbara and Peter went out to look for the other ghosts. They fetched in the poor Mad Monk and laid him on the refectory table and then they went to the burial mound to find Aunt Hortensia. Because ectoplasm is made of nothingness and you can't get rid of nothing, exorcism often makes ghosts go solid before destroying them. Aunt Hortensia, who always seemed to do things more than other people, hadn't just gone solid, she'd gone like granite. Her neck stump was like one of those poles that firemen slide down to get to fires quickly, and as they dragged her along the castle corridors her bunions gave off a clanging, metallic sound.

Peter and Barbara found the Colourless Ladies

lying in a heap near the moat and Rick, stumbling across what seemed to be a gigantic, grey, dried-out dish cloth, found that he had stepped on Walter the Wet.

One of their worst sights was the Shuk, lying on his back with his legs in the air and blood coming out of his mouth from trying to carry Aunt Hortensia's stone-hard head. All his tails had gone, his eye was closed and when Rick lifted him he whined with pain. As for the Head itself, Barbara couldn't lift it; she had to dribble it into the castle like a football.

The children had never worked so hard as they did that night. They found an old tin bath which someone had left on the rocket site and put Walter in to soak. Barbara dressed the Mad Monk's boils and Peter screamed and screamed at the buttery mess which had been George to see if he could get him to scream back. They massaged Aunt Hortensia's stump till their fingers ached, rubbed the Ladies with different coloured moulds and lichens to see if they could get their colours back and made poultices for Ughtred and Grimbald who were doubled up with stomach cramps.

Though she was still so weak, the Hag was wonderful. 'Say Latin curses over him backwards,' she advised Barbara as the Mad Monk groaned in pain. Or; 'There's some dried wormwood in the larder; try that on the Shuk's tail.'

But though they never stopped for a minute, though Humphrey did everything to make himself useful, it seemed for a while as if most of the ghosts were too ill to recover. And then:

'Oh, children!' screamed the Hag, the tears absolutely *rushing* down her nose. 'Oh look! Oh, Hamish. My husband! My Gliding Kilt!'

Rushing over, they saw a rusty sword begin to form itself very slowly and waveringly in the air. For a while, the sword just hung there patiently, waiting. Then slowly a wound appeared, gaping and bloody, and round it a torn shirt and some skin – and then with a relieved 'whoosh' the sword dropped down into the chest. The Gliding Kilt's face came next, then his arms, and lastly his knee stumps peering out below the kilt like young asparagus tips pushing through the earth.

'Hamish! Oh, Hamish,' said the Hag, and as she took him in her arms the room filled suddenly and gloriously with the smell of mouldering pig's intestine.

It must have been a sort of magic time limit when the effect of the exorcism began to wear off because Peter jumped up as the skull he was holding began to scream softly. One tail reappeared on the Shuk's back, then two, then three. . . .

'Oh look!' said Humphrey. 'Winifred's bowl's back! Winnie! Winnie, your bowl!'

A Colourless Lady turned blue, another showed patches of green. The Grey Lady got up and began at once to totter about looking for her teeth.

'Head?' said Aunt Hortensia's stump, and when they brought her head to her they saw that it was almost back to its old, disgusting, white-haired nothingness.

This happy scene was suddenly and terribly interrupted by a shriek of anguish as Sucking Susie, followed by the four vampire boys, came flapping into the room.

'My Baby, my Rose,' howled Susie, quite beside herself. 'She's dead, she's dead, she's DEAD!'

A complete and frightful silence fell in the Castle Hall.

'No,' gasped the Hag weakly.

Rick had gone deathly white. 'No,' he said also. '*No*!'

But as he stepped forward and took the tiny, grey body from Susie's claws it seemed there could be no doubt. Rose had shrunk almost to nothingness – she hardly stretched across the palm of his hand. Her body was quite cold and completely still. There was no heartbeat.

'*No*,' said Rick again. He was trembling all over but with a tremendous effort he managed to steady himself. Then he bent over and very gently pulled Rose's thread of a mouth open with his hand.

'The kiss of life?' whispered Barbara.

Rick didn't answer. He lifted Rose up in his cupped hands and began to breathe into her mouth. In – out; in – out; in – out. . . .

Nothing. No movement. No one stirred in the Castle Hall. Only a small, stifled sob from Humphrey the Horrible broke the silence.

Still Rick breathed softly, steadily, never stopping, holding Rose's jaw open with his fingertips.

'It's no good,' wailed Sucking Susie, beating her wings hysterically. 'She's dead, I tell you, she's dead, she's dead.'

Rick didn't even look up. He just went on quietly, steadily breathing. In and out, in and out. . . .

And then suddenly the limp, cold thing in his hand gave a tiny jerk, so faint that he thought he had imagined it. Then another; a little twitch, a judder and . . . yes, it was her heart. It was beating. She was *alive*.

'Oh *heck*,' said Rick the Rescuer, completely disgusted. Because from his own eyes it must have been, there'd dropped on to the little body a fat, wet, and quite unmistakable tear.

Seventeen

After that, of course, there was only one thing to do. 'A party!' said the Hag. She was still full of aches and pains, the Gliding Kilt's left thumb was still missing but the Hag *loved* parties and couldn't resist giving them.

Rick went out to see if Peregrine wanted to come but he had fallen asleep in the cockpit of the Cherokee, so they just covered him with a blanket and left him there.

There is nothing like release from danger to make you feel ecstatically and wonderfully gay. Outside, the owls hooted and a baleful moon glared through the scudding clouds. Inside, the ghosts ate toadskin rissoles, stewed spookfish and minced gall bladder, and showed each other their exorcism scars.

'Are you *sure* you don't want me to make you any maggot sandwiches?' the Hag kept asking the children. 'It would be no trouble at all.'

But Rick and Barbara and Peter said they were perfectly happy with the chocolate and apples they'd brought from the plane.

As the night went on, everyone got merrier and merrier. Rick was surprised to see a fat bull seal among the guests but when he tried to walk through him to help the Hag serve drinks, he went sprawling over his very solid body.

'That's Henry,' Sucking Susie explained. 'Rose's Dinner. He's so fond of her he won't let any of the other seals feed her at all.'

The Gliding Kilt's thumb appeared just after midnight and then a *very* nice thing happened. The Grey Lady found her teeth. At least she *said* they were her teeth and they were certainly a very good fit. She'd just glided out to get some air and was quite carelessly turning over the earth on Aunt Hortensia's burial mound and there they were!

Everybody was very happy for her and no one said that perhaps it was a bit *unlikely* when she'd died three hundred miles away on the Isle of Man that her teeth would turn up in the north of Scotland but as Aunt Hortensia's head wisely said: 'When all's said and done, teeth are teeth!'

And of course when they'd eaten and drunk and played games and managed to persuade the Finnish harp-playing ghost that she was still too weak to give a concert on the clifftop, they all got to their feet and drank the toast that the ghosts always drank now when they were together.

'Rick the Rescuer!'

But though Rick was very pleased, this time he decided to make a speech himself. 'Ladies, gentlemen, ghosts and seals,' he said, leaping up on to the table. 'I would like to say something about my friend, Humphrey.'

Everybody looked at Humphrey who was playing with Baby Rose and his ectoplasm turned dark pink from pleasure and embarrassment.

'If Humphrey had not come to fetch us there

would be no Henderson Ghost Sanctuary. And no ghosts.'

Everyone looked at everyone else, and Aunt Hortensia's head nodded so hard that the Shuk dropped it.

'Humphrey was ill and weak but he glided all those many, many miles to get help. Ladies, Gentlemen, Seals and Ghosts,' said Rick, getting excited and waving his arms. 'Humphrey may not be Horrible. In fact if you want my opinion, Humphrey will never be Horrible. But Humphrey is something *better* than Horrible. Humphrey is *Heroic*.'

There was a short silence while the ghosts took this in. Then a great beam of pride passed across the faces of the Hag and the Gliding Kilt while the whole hall full of ghosts rose to their feet, raised their glasses of rats' blood and thundered with a single voice: 'HUMPHREY THE HEROIC!'

After that, the good-byes could not be postponed any longer. It only lacked another hour till dawn and the children had their way back to make.

They were just starting the long round of hugs and kisses when something most extraordinary happened. First a kind of chill passed through the hall. An owl screeched. And then, there appeared in one of the high, arched windows, a ghost that none of them had ever seen before.

He was not a very nice-looking ghost. Even when he'd been alive he'd been horrid to look at. Now, he was undoubtedly a mess.

'Can . . . Can I come in?' stammered Lord

135

Bullhaven. (He had woken up in the hotel with a swollen jaw and in such a fiendish temper that he'd left the clergymen and Professor Brassnose stranded, leapt into his car and driven away at ninety miles an hour – straight into a stone wall.)

There was a stunned silence. Then:

'You!' shrieked the Hag, going through the roof.

'Ghost Murderer,' yelled the Mad Monk.

'Exorcist!' roared the Gliding Kilt.

'The nerve of it, coming here!' shouted Aunt Hortensia's head.

Lord Bullhaven's ghost stood waveringly on the windowsill. Then it seemed to shrink into itself and began slowly to turn away.

And then, once again, Rick leapt on to the table.

'Ghosts of Britain, I'm *ashamed* of you,' he said. 'Did I or did I not tell you what a sanctuary is?'

The ghosts looked up at him, silent and ashamed.

'A sanctuary is a place of safety. For *everyone*. I admit that when he was alive, Lord Bullhaven was a total and unutterable pig.'

Lord Bullhaven's ghost, on the windowsill, nodded sadly.

'But after all you weren't all that wonderful when you were alive yourselves, were you? What about Henry the Eighth's housekeeping money – was it *really* a mistake?' he said, looking at Aunt Hortensia's stump which blushed crimson. 'And why was the Mad Monk walled up alive in the first place, have you asked him that? And what about all the people the Gliding Kilt killed in the Battle of Otterburn?'

'That was a *battle*.'

136

'It was still killing,' said Rick sternly. 'Ghosts of Britain, I *appeal* to you to forget Lord Bullhaven's past and open this sanctuary to every spook or ghoul or wraith or lost spirit in need of a place to lay his head.'

For a moment there was silence. Then the ghosts, deeply moved by his words, moved forward towards the window.

'Welcome to Insleyfarne, Lord Bullhaven,' said the Gliding Kilt.

And with a sob of gratitude, the wicked spectre flew down and stretched out his gory hands in greeting.

When the children got back to the plane they found poor Peregrine standing sadly beside the engine and looking out to sea. He'd woken up without remembering anything that had happened and had absolutely no idea how he'd come to land his aeroplane on a cold grey beach in the middle of nowhere. There didn't seem to be any way of explaining either, so they just spoke to him gently and told him to fly back home which he was only too pleased to do.

In the plane Rick was very silent. Saying good-bye to the ghosts had made him feel completely hollow and though the Hag had promised that Humphrey could come and haunt Norton Castle School in the spring, he felt flat and tired and grey.

Barbara looked at him quietly for a moment. Then she leant forward. 'Before we came away I was reading about the polar bears,' she yelled in his ear. 'The ones in Alaska.'

Rick nodded. 'What about them?'

'They're in a very bad way. Becoming very rare. Extinct perhaps. Rich people go and hunt them from aeroplanes and snowmobiles. It's perfectly disgusting.'

Rick was still silent but his face had changed. He was working things out. How soon could he get to Alaska, how much would it cost? Should he take Barbara and Peter or go alone? What exactly did polar bears eat?

Barbara watched him for a while. Then she leant back, satisfied. He'd be all right now. For a boy like Rick, there is always something important to do.